D0486092

THE BAR CODE TATTOO

Also by Suzanne Weyn

The Bar Code Rebellion

The Bar Code Prophecy

Reincarnation

Distant Waves: A Novel of the Titanic

Empty

The Invisible World: A Novel of the Salem Witch Trials

AUG 15

THE BAR CODE TATTOO

SUZANNE WEYN

SCHOLASTIC INC.

THIS BOOK IS THE PROPERTY OF
THE NATIONAL CITY PUBLIC LIBRARY
1401 NATIONAL CITY BLVD
NATIONAL CITY, CA 91950

*— With love to
Diana, Rae, and Bill Gonzalez*

*And with deepest thanks to Tisha Hamilton,
David Levithan, and David Young for being
so generous with their brilliance
in helping me create this story
— Suzanne Weyn*

If you purchased this book without a cover, you should be aware that this book is stolen property. It was reported as "unsold and destroyed" to the publisher, and neither the author nor the publisher has received any payment for this "stripped book."

No part of this publication may be reproduced, stored in a retrieval system, or transmitted in any form or by any means, electronic, mechanical, photocopying, recording, or otherwise, without written permission of the publisher. For information regarding permission, write to Scholastic Inc., Attention: Permissions Department, 557 Broadway, New York, NY 10012.

ISBN 978-0-545-47054-4

Copyright © 2004 by Suzanne Weyn. All rights reserved. Published by Scholastic Inc. SCHOLASTIC and associated logos are trademarks and/or registered trademarks of Scholastic Inc.

12 11 10 9 8 7 6 5 4   13 14 15 16/0

Printed in the U.S.A.   40
This edition first printing, October 2012
Book design by Steve Scott
The text type was set in Utopia.

THE NATIONAL CITY PUBLIC LIBRARY
1401 NATIONAL CITY BLVD
NATIONAL CITY, CA 91950

PART 1

"... everything can be taken from a man but one thing: the last of the human freedoms — to choose one's attitude in any given circumstance, to choose one's own way."

Viktor E. Frankl
Man's Search for Meaning

CHAPTER 1

Outside, rain drummed against the window. Across the metal desk, the guidance counselor talked. Talked and talked. The light in his office was way too bright.

She'd absorbed his bad news fifteen minutes ago. *Time for you to shut up now*, she thought. But he kept on talking.

He shook his head, full of sympathy manufactured for the moment. She didn't buy it as genuine. He barely knew her. How bad could he really feel?

"Sorry, Kayla," he said. "I haven't seen an art scholarship issued to a student weak in computer skills for the last five years, definitely not since 2020. You shouldn't expect to get one, or even to be accepted at the art schools you've applied to. That's just how it is."

Mr. Kerr tugged on his sleeve and her eyes locked onto the inch-long rectangular patch of straight black lines on the underside of his left wrist.

A bar code tattoo.

This wasn't the first time she'd seen one, of course. This year all the kids in her grade turned seventeen, the age when a person qualified for a bar code. As soon as their birthdays came, the first thing they did was run out and get tattooed. Everyone — even adults — was getting one. Both of Kayla's parents had been tattooed for seven months now.

Even though she saw tattoos everywhere, they continued to fascinate her. How bizarre to be branded like a box of cereal. Didn't people mind being counted as just one more product on a shelf? There had to be more to a person than that.

Unaware of Kayla's gaze on his wrist, the guidance counselor kept talking.

Outside, the rain kept pounding. She twisted in her chair to see it better. Rivers of water raced across the glass.

And then Kayla . . .

* * *

A jet streaks by. It's low and she's never seen one that looks exactly like it. She's in the woods outside a great city. Tall white buildings spire to the sky. A thick shining wall surrounds the city, about fifteen feet high. Someone else is with her. She senses him standing behind, but doesn't turn to see.

Near the wall, people walk toward the city. Many people. Her heartbeat quickens. A low rumble, like many voices speaking at once, fills her mind. She smiles.

* * *

She blinked hard. Mr. Kerr was no longer talking. The only sound was rain. The guidance counselor stared at her from across his desk.

"Sorry," she apologized to him, with a quick, stressed, half smile. *What was that about?* she wondered.

"So you understand what I've been saying?" he asked.

She nodded. She'd understood it a billion minutes ago when he first began — the art world had no place for a talented artist with bad computer-skill grades.

That's what it amounted to, though of course he felt compelled to subject her to the *entire* explanation. Although she was only half listening, she understood.

The explanation went more or less like this: Only a few of the most experienced artists were required to input drawings into computer art data banks. These computer-generated images were used to create all other artwork. No art school would award a scholarship to a student weak in data imaging — a student like her.

When she'd first realized what he was telling her, she'd felt like a figure in a video game.

Smash! A direct hit!

Kayla Reed — blown to smithereens.

Game Over! Game Over! Game Over!

Bye-bye.

Maybe she wasn't completely out, though. It deserved at least a fight on her part. *Here goes, what the hell.* Leaning forward, she reached across his desk and tapped on the computer screen that displayed her grades. "My art marks are all Achievement Plus. Holographic Web Design — AP. MTML Advanced — AP. I even took an extra credit in Acid Full Loop Advanced on my own time so I could add my own soundtracks to my art. That counts, doesn't it?"

"I understand that, but look at these computer grades," he countered. "Computer Concepts — Insufficient Mastery Achieved. Computer Methods — IMA. Data Collecting — IMA. All these IMAs in computer just don't impress schools. In fact, if you get one more IMA, you might not even graduate next year."

"But that stuff has *nothing* to do with art. I suppose I should have attended more regularly. But it's so boring. They can test me — I already know most of it," she fought back.

"Not an option, I'm afraid."

"What if I got recommendations from my design teachers? They all say I've got lots of talent. I've been art-tracked since ninth grade. I would go outside and draw during computer class. No one cares if you can draw, I know. But still . . . it has more to do with art than computers do."

"Kayla, it's my job to make you aware of how the schools will view the situation," he said, and she noticed something in his eyes that seemed to shut down. He wasn't going to do anything for her.

She stood. "Thank you for letting me know . . . all this." She really had to get out of his office. She needed a place to scream, cry, and maybe kick something.

He rose, too. "You could still be accepted into an art college without a scholarship. Is that a possibility for you?"

"Not likely," she replied.

"Too bad you didn't apply for a Global-1 Federal Grant at the beginning of the year," he said.

"Things were a lot different for me then," she told him. Warnings flashed in her mind. *I don't want to go in this direction. Change the subject.* Talking about the situation at home was too upsetting. Besides, it was none of his business.

"Oh?" he asked. "Are there problems at home? Is there anything you'd like to talk about?" His eyes became warm with more of that instant sympathy.

He extended his arms in a gesture meant to be helpful, embracing. It hiked up his sleeve and Kayla glanced again at the row of straight lines tattooed on the underside of his wrist.

Since he had the bar code, could he tell her why it had driven her father into a depression so deep that he didn't even bother to go to work anymore?

"The tattoo," she began. "How do you like it?"

He appeared puzzled. It wasn't what he'd expected her to say. Then his face relaxed into a smile. "It's convenient, I suppose. All my banking and identification numbers are encoded right here. If I were rushed to the hospital, billing and medical information would be right at hand." He smiled. "No pun intended."

She smiled back politely. "But don't they get all that information from an eye scan now?" she asked. These days eye scans did everything. They unlocked doors, identified you to your computer, and even proved your identity at airports.

"An eye scan only proves that you're you," Mr. Kerr pointed out. "It doesn't contain all your other information."

He clearly approved of his tattoo and was clueless as to why it had blown away her father — just as clueless as Kayla herself. Sure, the tattoo was impersonal and, she thought, demeaning. But her father had known all that before he'd gotten it. What had happened afterward? — this is what she wanted to know. What had left him so freaked?

"Is there more you'd like to talk about?" Mr. Kerr asked. "Anything else you'd like to know?"

Nothing you *can tell me*, she thought. "No. Thank you." With a parting nod, she headed into the empty hallway, not sure what to do next.

No art school.

There it was — the simple reality.

All her life she'd assumed she'd go to an art college or a design school. She had a box full of ribbons, certificates, and other prizes for her art. She'd spent every summer at the Art Institute at Garrison drawing and painting as well as learning all the new technologies. But this was the last summer of high school, the last summer that she'd be eligible for the program. She'd always figured she'd go to art school and then get a job with the government in the Public Murals Program. But they only took students from the top twenty art schools. What was she supposed to do now?

The hallway was empty. In a few minutes, though, class change tones would sound, releasing a flood of students into the halls. This meeting with Mr. Kerr had run into her lunch period, but she had zero appetite and didn't want to see anyone. Instead, she walked to the nearest stairwell, a quiet place to hide from everything.

She sat and the stairs felt cold through her neon-blue pants. Her straight brown, cobalt-blue-streaked hair swung forward as she rested her chin on her hands.

Sitting there, with the rain still pounding on the windows, she fell into a world of private pictures. They floated before her in no particular order. Snaps of conversation. Images of figures against sunlight. Individual movie screens hurtling through the inner space of her mind. That was how she usually thought things through — in pictures, not words.

She saw her father staring at the bar code on his wrist. His dark eyes staring emptily.

Another image floated by — her mother's

mouth forming words. "Joe, why aren't you at work? They'll fire you if you don't go in."

Then an earlier picture, a better one — an image of him sitting at the side of Kayla's bed at night. He was reading *Harry Potter and the Sorcerer's Stone* and had come to the part where Voldemort's evil helper was revealed to Harry. "It's true," her father had said thoughtfully, putting down his e-reader for a moment. "It isn't always easy to recognize your true enemy."

She turned at the sound of footsteps. A tall, slim guy carried a stack of books down the stairs above her. He had black, close-cut hair and brown skin. The top book tumbled and bounced down the stairs. She jumped out of its way.

"Whoa. Sorry! You okay?" he asked, hurrying down to her.

"Yeah. Okay." She looked into his eyes — hazel marbled with vivid green. She knew who he was — everyone at Winfrey High did. Mfumbe Taylor had represented their school in the first Virtual Global Teen *Jeopardy*. He'd won, too.

As he picked up his book, he looked up at her. "Hey, you're *not* okay."

She realized for the first time that her eyes and cheeks were wet. She'd been crying and hadn't even known it.

"Did the book hit you?" he asked.

"No." She used her thumb to wipe smeared mascara from her face.

He fished a stick of gum from his pocket and offered it to her. "Want some? It always makes *me* feel better."

Kayla took the piece and popped it into her mouth. Peppermint. It *did* make her feel better, but maybe it was his concern that worked the trick.

"Are you sure you're okay?" he checked.

She looked up at him without answering. For some reason she felt a strong, nearly overwhelming urge to tell him everything that was wrong — about her parents, the lost chance at art school, everything. But that would have been too strange — she didn't even know him.

"Yeah, I'm fine," she said.

"Okay, well, I've got to get these books to the library," he said, backing away. "You know if they're late, they'll send the library squad."

She smiled. "I know. Thanks for the gum."

"Sure." He waved and entered the flow of kids who were returning from lunch. All she really wanted now was to cut her last classes and go home. Moving quickly, her head down so she'd make no eye contact with anyone, she headed to her locker.

It was in sight when a voice shouted from behind her.

"Kayla, I've been looking all over for you."

Her shoulders hunched. Caught!

CHAPTER 2

"You've got to come with me right now!" Her friend Amber Thorn wrapped her fingers around Kayla's wrist and began to pull her toward the girls' room across the hall. "I have something amazing to show you."

"Can it wait?" Kayla asked.

"Hey! What's wrong?" Amber didn't miss a thing. "You've been crying. Come on." Kayla stared into Amber's vivid blue black-rimmed eyes and let a resigned sigh escape. Nothing would stop her, so there was no sense in trying.

Inside the girls' room, they sat on the metal bench against the tiled wall and Kayla told Amber her bad news. "It would have been nice if someone had let me know all these computer requirements would be important," she complained. "I could have worked a little harder on my computer grades. I mean, you'd think one of my art teachers or a guidance counselor would have mentioned it."

"This is *not* fair!" Amber cried, tossing back her metallic-silver curls indignantly. "You're the most talented artist I know. You can actually draw. How many other kids can do that? With them it's all computer imagery."

Amber was the most loyal friend imaginable and Kayla loved her for it. She knew that even if she could draw only a stick figure, Amber would say that stick-figure drawing was the truest kind of art and that Kayla was an artistic genius who drew the best stick figures.

"Thanks, Amber," she said. "But nobody cares anymore if you can draw or paint. And anyway, it doesn't matter because without a scholarship I'm blown up. Dad hasn't worked in over a month and I don't know when he's going back. My mother thinks he might already have been fired and doesn't want to tell us. If that's true, I don't know what kind of money they can give me for college. Tuitions are astronomical. God, you have to be a zillionaire's kid just to go to college."

"Really," Amber seconded. "My dad keeps yelling about scholarships but I'm never getting one. You have to be a brain or at least talented for that."

"You're talented," Kayla insisted.

"At what?" Amber demanded to know.

"Well . . . you're a great friend. And you're pretty."

"I don't think they give scholarships for those things," Amber reminded her. "The Beauty Scholarship has been discontinued for decades."

"Then there's two of us without a scholarship," Kayla said.

"But speaking of the bar code," Amber began.

"We weren't," Kayla pointed out.

"Oh, then say we were," she replied. She lifted her stretchy pink sleeve, pushing it above her elbow to reveal a curved reddish-brown line snaking up her arm. It coiled off in winding branches festooned with exotic flower designs. Every few inches, the garlands split, curling off in ever more winding, complex designs, continuing up her forearm.

Elaborately beautiful as it was, Kayla could only stare at one particular part of Amber's mehndi body art — the rigid, parallel black lines by her wrist, partly hidden within the design.

"When did you get it?" she asked, stunned.

"You mean the 'too?"

Kayla nodded.

"This morning, first thing. I went straight to the post office before the line got too long."

"Did it hurt?" Kayla asked.

"The bar code? No, they do it with laser beams. It only hurts when they jab your finger to draw blood." She examined her left thumb. "The needle didn't even leave a mark, though."

"Why do they need your blood?" Kayla couldn't see what blood had to do with a tattoo.

Amber shrugged. "Don't know. Maybe they do it so they can list your blood type on your medical records. Afterward, I went right across the street to the body-art guy and had this done. Everyone's doing it. Look how he worked the bar code into the design. The scanner only picks up the code, so it doesn't matter if something is drawn over it. The design lasts at least three months. Isn't it final level?"

"It *is*," Kayla had to agree. "The art is really final level. He's a guy who's found a way to make money by drawing."

"You could do something like that," Amber suggested. "Be a body artist."

"I had something better in mind than living in the back of a crummy little store or in a tent going from fair to fair," Kayla said.

The tone for next class sounded and took their attention from Amber's mesmerizing arm. "Happy birthday, by the way," Kayla said as they stood up from the bench. "I'll give you your gift tonight at your party."

"Tell me. What is it?"

Kayla grinned. "You'll see. Don't worry. You'll love it."

Amber studied her arm again as they left the bathroom. "You don't really like the tattoo, do you?"

"I like the body art. But the bar code creeps me."

"You've never liked new things. You've always been that way. You'll get used to it, though. It's really great. My junior license is in here. If I get stopped I just have to show the cop my wrist. He runs his little handheld scanner over it, and off I go."

"But why does it have to be tattooed on?" Kayla insisted. "Why can't you just carry a card?"

"Oh, come on," Amber scoffed. "Cards always get lost or stolen. Terrorists and thieves are constantly stealing your identity or some stupid thing like that. Nobody likes identity chips, either. They've been pushing those practically since we were born but they have to be buried under your skin. Ew! This is so much better. There's nothing hard stuck in your arm. It's perfect. I can never lose it — and you know how bad I am about losing stuff."

Kayla smiled. That was for sure.

"Do you have to change the tattoo when your final license comes through?" Kayla asked.

"No, of course not. The *file* changes, not the bar code."

That meant that somewhere — who knew where? — there was a big data entry on everyone who had the bar code. A file that constantly changed as your life changed.

Kayla imagined banks and banks of dronelike workers at computers — tracking people, checking their records, and sending the information back to some central data bank, constantly updating and revising. Did they ever leave their computer screens? Could there ever be a moment when they were changing shifts, when some piece of information could slip by them? What if people weren't even involved? Maybe computers just zapped information back and forth across a vast network of circuitry, reporting your life as if it were just data.

"Everyone has a file," Amber said. "There's been a file on everyone for years."

"But people haven't always *worn* their files," Kayla argued.

Amber shrugged, unconcerned. "What's the difference? Walk me to class."

"I'm going home," Kayla told her.

"Why?"

"School feels like a cage today. I can't sit still."

"You'd better not get caught."

"I never do."

The moving walkway carried Kayla along the length of the huge shopping mall. She was there to get the holographic audio chip by Amber's favorite group, Lunar Tick. Its release date coincided with Amber's birthday, so Kayla had to wait until this afternoon to buy it.

The frigid piped-in air made her shiver. The rain had soaked her as she ran from the bulletbus station into the mall. She imagined ice crystallizing in her sopping-wet hair.

She began walking faster than the walkway. The urgent need to get home was still with her, but this had to be done first.

Was this urge an intuition or just anxiety about her awful day, a need to get home and hide away? Kayla couldn't always tell. All her life she'd had little warnings, premonitions about what was to come. Sometimes the premonitions really came true. But other times, they didn't. So, she'd learned not to pay too much attention to them.

As she went along, she gazed absently into the glass fronts of the stores she passed. In every one, she saw people presenting their wrists to cashiers in payment for their purchases. Occasionally, one or two paid with e-cards. The cashiers looked annoyed when this happened.

At the media store Harmonic Spheres — as in most other stores — they took special minors' debit e-cards. The money she spent would be taken from an account her parents had set up for her. This was necessary since paper money and coins had been replaced with e-cards over the last five years.

Finally, she stepped off the walkway. The Lunar Tick display was right there in front of Harmonic Spheres. The postage-stamp-sized chip plugged into a holographic laser player that was as thin as an e-card.

Kayla stood at the front of the store to watch the twelve-inch musicians gyrate on top of the laser player as they performed their new release, *Home to Mars*. Amber would flip.

The chip came in a case with cover art that showed the band members hurtling through space, headed toward Mars. Kayla could easily figure out how it was accomplished. An image of Mars electronically clipped from a website, cleverly overlaid with digital images of the band members, and then placed on a digital space background. Swirl around some neon paint effects, select a font for the titles, and there you were — instant art. Simple to do, but the idea was clever. Maybe that's what art was now, coming up with amusing visual concepts. If so, she could do that. Her mind was full of images.

At the counter, she presented her minors' debit e-card. The young salesclerk glanced at the birth date. "You won't be using this much longer," he noted. He pushed up his sleeve and presented his bar code tattoo. "Pretty soon you'll have one of these."

"Yeah. Sure," Kayla mumbled as he handed her the bagged chip.

Kayla got off the GlobalTrac bulletbus on a residential street of narrow, attached row houses. The downpour had subsided to a drizzle. On the sidewalk, puddles reflected the orange glow of sunset, spinning it around in their oily pools.

Heading toward her house, she saw that people had gathered in a group ahead of her, so she quickened her pace, going even faster as she realized that they were standing in front of her yard. A siren blared and an ambulance sped past, its red light spinning.

It stopped abruptly at the bottom of her driveway. She ran toward it, splashing through puddles. The crowd by her house was thick, forming a wall between her and her front walk. Frantic, she pushed through the barrier of people.

She was nearly to the front when a strong hand gripped her shoulder. A face became distinct, emerging from the blur of faces. It was Gene. In his late twenties, Gene lived with two roommates in the house next door. "I heard your mother screaming and ran over," he told her, his eyes wild with the urgency of his story. "But your front door was locked. Then the ambulance pulled up. I think it has to do with your father."

Kayla broke free of Gene's grasp and pushed her way to the front. Then she stopped short. Paramedics bent over her father, who lay on the ground on a stretcher, his eyes shut. A sheet lay on top of him.

Terror punched the breath from her chest. He was so white! She stood, staring, paralyzed by a terrible feeling of unreality.

His eyes darted right to left beneath closed lids. Realizing he wasn't dead, she lunged to his side. "Dad," she cried. A paramedic tucked the sheet tightly around him and she saw there was blood on it. "Dad! It's me!"

His lids lifted a fraction, then relaxed. "We have to take him." The paramedic spoke to her as he gripped one end of the stretcher and his partner took the other.

Her mother raced out of the house, her face wet with tears, her dark hair tangled.

"Ashley," called their neighbor, Mrs. Fern. "What happened?"

Ashley Reed's mouth opened to answer, but she spotted her daughter and seemed to forget what she was about to say. "Come on, Kayla," she said, wrapping her arm around Kayla's shoulder and guiding her toward the ambulance.

"What happened, Mom?" Kayla asked.

Her mother's hands covered her face and she suddenly shook violently. "The bar code . . ." she gasped through her tears. "The bar code did this to him."

OBITUARY NOTICE FOR JOSEPH REED

Tribune E-Journal, March 18, 2025

FBI researcher Joseph Reed, 47, died on Monday, March 16, of self-inflicted wounds. The deceased's wife, Ashley Reed, reported that her husband had been depressed ever since he was passed over for a promotion at the bureau three months prior to his suicide. She had urged him to seek professional counseling, but claims her husband refused. Mr. Reed is survived by his wife and their 16-year-old daughter, Kayla Marie Reed.

CHAPTER 3

Kayla stared down at the red splotches in the tub. No cleanser or formula she'd attempted in the last ten days had been able to erase them. And her mother was in no shape to do anything about it.

Kayla didn't particularly want to clean her father's blood from the tub, either. It felt disloyal, somehow, like wiping away the last bit of him. But how could she use the tub or shower again with such a hideous reminder in front of her? She couldn't shower at Amber's house forever. This was their only bathroom.

The stains had collected around the drain, probably pooling there when the bloodstained water had been drained out. The faucet dripped and her eyes locked onto the falling quicksilver drops. Counting the drips, one by one, one after the other, she drifted farther away . . .

*   *   *

The people continue to move toward the city. The person behind her puts his hand on her shoulder. He speaks to her and she hears his words in her head. His words are louder and clearer than the rumble of conversation she hears from the other people. "Let's go," he says.

* * *

Mrs. Reed stepped into the bathroom and Kayla startled back to the present. Why was she having these waking visions? What did they mean?

Though normally she would have already left for work, Mrs. Reed still wore her bathrobe, and her eyes were smudged with the old eye makeup she hadn't removed since yesterday. "Aren't you late?" Kayla asked.

"They'll get by without me for a little while longer," she answered, staring in the mirror, seeming mesmerized by her own disheveled reflection. In Kayla's opinion, the maternity unit where her mother worked as a nurse would probably function *better* without her — at least lately.

Mrs. Reed turned on the faucet and began washing her hands, but the washing motions soon climbed up to her wrist. Her movements quickened and her entire body grew tense and agitated. Grabbing a nailbrush from the sink, she scrubbed the bar code tattoo on her wrist, each stroke becoming increasingly violent.

Kayla pushed in front of her and shut the tap. "That's *not* going to get the tattoo off," she yelled. This crazy washing ritual had become a daily event. It unnerved Kayla. She needed her mother to stay strong for her, not to turn into the twisted bundle of nerves she'd become.

"That bar code killed your father," her mother said dully. "I want it off of me."

Kayla wanted to shake her mother. How many times was she going to repeat that awful statement without explaining? "Why do you keep saying that?" she asked. "Tell me what you mean."

"It's better if you don't know," her mother answered.

"How can it be better?"

"It is. Believe me, it is."

"I can't talk to you," Kayla shouted. The overload of frustration was suddenly unbearable. She couldn't even bear to stand next to her mother. How had she become so pathetic?

Kayla banged the door back as she stormed into the hallway. At the stair landing, she stood, breathing heavily with anger and frustration.

It was just the two of them now. Her father had always been the parent she could talk to. But he'd abandoned them. For some inconceivable reason of his own, he'd just decided to go. For good. Now it felt as if her mother were abandoning her, too.

Air. She needed air. It was as if her father had breathed it all up with his last dying breaths.

She raced down the stairs and directly out the front door. She didn't stop until she reached the titanium wall that separated all the front yards from the sidewalk. She leaned heavily on it as she watched life go by — people walking, cars passing.

Next door, Gene sat on his steps in a T-shirt and cutoff shorts. He tossed a small ball to his brown-and-white terrier, then turned to Kayla and waved. As his dog raced after the ball, Gene got up and joined Kayla by the gate, staying on his side of the front yard.

"Everything okay?" he asked with his eye on the dog.

"I guess," she said, dismayed that her voice shook. She didn't really know him, not well enough to tell him her problems. He shared the house with two other guys about his age. They all worked down at the post office, which was now actually a Global-1 office.

The United States Postal Service had gone bankrupt about ten years ago. People agreed that its financial collapse was mostly due to the Internet. No one needed stamps anymore and people usually used a faster private carrier to get the items they ordered off the net. It was no help that terrorist groups occasionally sent poisons, disease bacteria, and explosives through the mail.

That was when Global-1, the international affiliation of corporations and individual billionaires, came to the rescue. They offered the government the funding to convert all postal buildings into government offices, with the provision that Global-1 would operate them. Many of the employees still felt loyal to Global-1 for saving their jobs, though the younger employees, like Gene and his friends, complained that Global-1 worked them hard and kept cutting their vacation time, health benefits, and overtime pay.

"How's your job?" she asked, mostly to fill the awkward silence that had arisen between them. Something about him always made her a little uncomfortable. It might have been the way he blinked his eyes just a little too often.

"I'm training for the 'too machine," he replied. His tone implied that this wasn't necessarily good news.

One of the most recent duties of postal workers was to administer the bar code tattoo. Certain employees received special training on how to work the small laser machine that imprinted the tattoo.

"How do you like it?"

He leaned closer to her and she detected cigarettes on his breathe. The smell repelled her. Almost no one smoked anymore, not in America. Ever since tobacco had been banned, the big tobacco companies had moved to Asia, where people continued to die of lung cancer by the millions.

"I hate it," he said. "That tattoo is evil."

Her heart raced. Did he know something?

"Why?" she asked, trying not to sound as eager for the answer as she was. If he knew something, she didn't want to make him uneasy about revealing it.

His eyes darted up and down the block and he waved her closer. "A few years ago, right after I got out of the army, I used to do tattoos, the regular ones, before they were outlawed. This was back a few years, when bar codes were big in Europe but were just starting up here. Guys from Europe were always coming in wanting their bar codes removed; women, too. They said regular dermatologists wouldn't do it because the laser lines went too deep into the layers of skin. My boss took them in back and I think he at least managed to mess the bar codes up. Naturally, I started to wonder why all these people wanted them off so bad."

"Did they ever say why?"

"Most of the time, no. One French guy, though, told me his life had gone downhill fast once he got his. *Undesirable* was the word he used. He said, 'It's like I turned into an *undesirable* overnight.'" Gene shrugged, as if the subject had begun to hurt his head and he wanted to get rid of it. "I don't know what's up with the bar codes, but I don't like being the guy who gives them out."

"Do you know what information they have stored in them?" Kayla asked quickly. She could see he was tiring of the topic and she didn't want to let him go before she learned something. "During your training, did they tell you?" Her heart picked up speed. They had to have told him *that*, at least.

"Not yet, but I know there's a database that tells you what's in that file. A friend of mine knows the password for the Global-1 info files. We're going to look into it when we've got the chance. I could get fired for hacking in. I start giving out bar codes on Monday. I've got to take a look, just for my own head, you know?"

"Sure. Would you tell me what you find out?"

Maybe she'd gone too far. Gene looked hesitant now. "I don't know about that," he said.

"It might help me to figure out why my father did . . . you know . . . what he did."

Gene stretched out his arm and displayed his bar code. "I hope there's nothing too awful in there, because I got one. Had to or be fired."

Before he could say more, his terrier, ball in jaws, pawed at his pant leg. "Cut it out!" he scolded, shaking the dog loose. The dog dropped the ball at his feet. Gene threw it back to the stoop and the dog raced after it. "You crazy dog," he shouted, following the dog back to his stoop without even saying good-bye to Kayla.

He's definitely strange, she thought, watching him stand by his front door and pull out a pack of cigarettes labeled in Chinese writing. But, strange or not, maybe he would learn something that could help her to figure out what was really contained in those formidable black strokes of the bar code.

Her mother appeared at the front door. She'd dressed in her white nurse's jumpsuit. Her chin-length hair was still unbrushed and knotty, and her eye makeup was still smudged. But at least she'd gotten out of her robe. "I'd like to talk to you," she said.

Kayla joined her at the door and they walked in together. They sat side by side on the living room couch. "I know I haven't really been there for you since your dad died," her mother admitted.

Kayla's hopes rose. Had her mother managed to grab hold of her emotions? Could she finally offer her daughter some support?

"You must understand," her mother went on, "this is complicated. I was the one who convinced Dad to get the bar code, and I was so wrong." She hung her head as tears welled. "I can't cope with what I did to him, to us. I killed him. I let it kill —"

"Please — tell me," Kayla pleaded. "Why do you think it killed him? How did it?"

Looking up again, her mother wiped her glistening eyes. "Just before he . . . died . . . I woke up in the middle of the night and he wasn't in bed. I found him at the computer. He didn't realize I was there at first but I watched him race through hundreds of bar codes and the files that went with them. He didn't have clearance for those files. He researched facts on places and things, not people. But somehow he'd gotten in."

"What was he looking for?" Kayla felt she had to find out.

"I don't know, but he stopped at one particular code profile and began to read it. He only got to read it for a few seconds before the screen went black. Some security blocker must have kicked in."

"Did you ask what he was doing?"

Mrs. Reed nodded. "But he wouldn't talk about it. We had a big fight over it. We were still angry and not speaking the day he cut . . . I need to lie down." She stood up unsteadily. "If the hospital calls, tell them I'll be there soon."

Kayla trailed her to the bottom of the stairs. "Don't walk away," she begged as her mother went up. "Tell me! Why do you think the bar code killed him?"

No reply came, just the sound of the bedroom door closing.

Kayla stopped at her locker for books and found a piece of peppermint gum taped to it. She knew who had put it there and it amazed her that a person she hardly knew at all had seen her pain. She glanced around to see if Mfumbe was near, but he wasn't.

Amber appeared at her side and smiled the too-bright smile she always wore lately. "How are you doing today?" she asked.

"Not bad."

"Not bad is good, right?" As they walked down the hall, Amber pulled some papers from her over-sized silver bag. "These are for you," she said, handing them to Kayla.

Kayla peered down at them, not understanding. She shot Amber a quizzical look.

"They're applications for your bar code," Amber said. "I knew you wouldn't get them on your own. Your birthday is in three weeks. You have to file now. You can thank me now or thank me later. Either way, you'll thank me."

Kayla thrust the papers back at Amber. "Thanks, but no thanks. I'm not getting it."

"Not getting it?" Amber shouted incredulously. "You can be as paranoid and suspicious as you like about it, but you have to realize that there's nothing you can do without a 'too! Nothing! For one thing, they don't give out any other kind of license anymore. No 'too, no license."

"That can't be true. They *have* to give another form of license other than one that's in a bar code," Kayla argued. "There's no law that says you have to get a bar code. Are you telling me that every single person who drives a car has a bar code tattoo?"

"Yes! Well, I don't know that for sure, but every driver I know has one. Good luck trying to get your hands on a license without it," Amber huffed. "You'll be like some kind of mutant freak. How are you going to pay for stuff?"

"I'll get an e-card."

Amber scoffed with a snort. "Yeah, like someone will really give an e-card to a seventeen-year-old. Plus it's such a higher level of difficulty to use one anymore. Salespeople get all banged out with you if you try. My grandmother tried to use hers the other day and it took so long, the other customers practically ran us out of the store." She shoved the application papers back at Kayla. "Take these. You'll need them."

"Thanks, but I don't want them," Kayla insisted, folding her arms and refusing to accept the applications. "My neighbor works for the post office. He told me that something's weird about the bar code. People are trying to take their 'toos off."

"Which one of those guys told you that?"

"Gene."

"That guy's a first-level flake," Amber said, rolling her eyes. "You would listen to *him*?"

"I know he'd odd, but he's training to work the bar code machine. He's got access to classified information."

"I bet he's lying," Amber said. "He's just trying to make himself look more important than he is."

As they rounded a corner, Kayla saw Mfumbe standing with a group of other seniors. His back was turned and he didn't notice her.

Amber pulled Kayla abruptly into a doorway. "If you *don't* get coded, you're going to wind up like" — she pointed at Mfumbe and his friends — "like them!"

"What's wrong with them?"

"Listen, I know you haven't really been paying attention to . . . well, to anything these last couple of weeks — and I completely understand — but how could you have missed *them*?"

"I talked to Mfumbe Taylor once."

Amber's face twisted in an expression of surprised disapproval. "Well, all I know about him is that he's a super brain. I guess he's okay. He aced that *Jeopardy* thing and all. I have no idea how he got mixed up with those others."

Kayla checked out Mfumbe's friends. They were all seniors, too. She knew who some of them were but had never really spoken to any of them.

Allyson Minor was one of those kids always hanging around in the science lab. Blond hair frizzled around her round face as if it were electrified by excess brain waves. She always wore baggy clothes — Kayla assumed it was to hide her weight.

Nedra Harris's short bright red hair was cut down to about a quarter-inch. It looked good on her because she was so slim and had such a delicate-featured face. A silver ring pierced her right eyebrow and she wore her angry attitude as though it were a matter of style.

The short heavyset guy with the dyed neon-orange hair was August Sanchez. He never said much in class, so Kayla didn't have much sense of what he was about. He was always dressed in khaki clothing that made her think of military uniforms. She knew he was a member of the Techno Club, which brought equipment into the classrooms.

Then Kayla focused on the one student she had never seen before. Her eyes widened as she surveyed his golden-brown eyes, thick brown hair, and high cheekbones. He was some exotic mix of ethnicities that she couldn't place. He smiled when he spoke to Nedra, and Kayla felt a sudden desperate desire to have him smile like that at her.

"He's out of this sphere, isn't he?" Amber noted.

"Totally final level," Kayla agreed. "Where did he come from?"

"Don't know. His name is Zekeal something. He just got here three weeks ago. When he showed up, this little clique sprung up around him. He's cute but I wouldn't go near him. He's involved with the same loser's deal as the rest of them."

"What deal is that?" Kayla asked.

"They're involved with some kind of campaign to get rid of bar code tattoos," Amber told her. "In fact, I think he's the head loser. He was the one who got them all going about it in the first place."

Now Kayla was completely interested.

She'd have to find out more about Zekeal. . . .

CHAPTER 4

Mfumbe turned and smiled when he noticed Kayla. "Will you sign our petition?" he asked.

Amber whispered fiercely in Kayla's ear, "No! Tell him no!"

"What's it about?" Kayla asked, pulling free of Amber's grip. Mfumbe presented her with a hand-held computer notebook with a short list of names that had been signed with the special pen attached to it.

"We're working with a senator named David Young on a campaign called Decode," Zekeal said, coming alongside Mfumbe. "Young wants serious curbs put on the bar code. He's working to pass laws that control where and when it can be used."

"Like on highways," Mfumbe added. "He's trying to pass a law prohibiting states from making bar codes a requirement at all tolls."

Amber came up behind Kayla. "What's wrong with that?" she challenged.

"Because the government could track your every move," Zekeal replied.

"If you haven't done anything wrong, who cares?"

"It's the principle of it," Mfumbe argued. "Our civil liberties have been shrinking ever since the turn of the last century. We lost a lot of civil rights because people became convinced it was the only way to stay safe. We've been losing more freedoms and rights ever since."

"I don't feel like that. I can do whatever I want," Amber argued back. "There are no freedoms I miss having. I haven't broken any laws, so I don't care who knows what about me. I have nothing to hide."

"You should have the freedom to travel without having your every move monitored by the government," Mfumbe replied. "Don't you agree to that?"

"I still say that if you have nothing to hide, you have nothing to worry about," Amber insisted. "Only criminals and terrorists need to worry about that."

"What if the British had been able to track George Washington during the revolution?" Mfumbe said. "Or what if slavers knew where runaways were on the Underground Railroad?"

"That's so over," Amber scoffed. "This is the twenty-first century."

"Maybe, but maybe it still applies. Besides, wouldn't you like to know what's in the bar code?" Mfumbe insisted. "What if there's stuff coded in there that isn't true?"

Amber waved him off dismissively. "You're so paranoid. I'm sure if something like that happened, you could find someone to call and have it fixed." She turned to Kayla. "We have to get to class."

"You go ahead," Kayla replied. "I want to hear more about this."

Amber shot Kayla an insistent look. "Kayla!" she urged.

"I'll be right there."

Amber rolled her eyes and hurried off down the hall.

"Your friend thinks you're making a big mistake," Mfumbe commented.

"Yeah, she's pretty banged out that I'm talking to you," Kayla said with a quick laugh. "She thinks you guys are crazy and dangerous."

"She's got a lot of company," Zekeal said.

"Thanks for the gum," she said quietly to Mfumbe.

He nodded. "How are you doing?"

"Been better." She wanted to get off this topic quickly. "Tell me more about Decode," she said.

"Zekeal's our Decode expert," Mfumbe said.

"All Senator Young is saying is that there should always be an alternative to the bar code. That way you're free to get the stupid tattoo or not get it," Zekeal told her. "It's simple, really."

Kayla reached for the petition and signed.

"Okay — an independent thinker!" Zekeal cheered.

Nedra appeared at his side and ran her hand along his arm. "I have to get to my locker. Are you coming?"

"Yeah, sure," he replied. Nedra tugged and he let her pull him away.

August and Allyson joined Mfumbe and Kayla. Allyson handed Kayla a magazine. "Check our 'zine, *KnotU2*," she offered. "It'll tell you about Decode."

"That's the name of our website, too," August added. He pushed some buttons on his small computer and the website opened just as the final morning tone sounded.

"Astral," Kayla said, impressed with the wildly colorful graphics. "I'll check it out on my computer later."

Kayla hurried to her class and slid into her seat just as her World Literature teacher was about to shut the door. Their assignment was to open the e-readers built into their desks and finish reading an article in the *Tribune E-Journal*. Instead, she folded the 'zine over her e-reader screen, flattened it, and began to read.

KnotU2
 be more than a cog in the machinery

First Your Food — Then Your Soul
By Allyson Minor
You all know Global-1 — the worldwide corporate superpower that has been unofficially controlling just about everything from behind the scenes since 2011. You know them because their

name is on everything from your cereal box to the high-speed bus you ride to school.

It's even on our country's leader. Our current president, billionaire Loudon Waters, was one of the founding members of Global-1. It's clear that he's only concerned about increasing Global-1's fortune and power. He couldn't care less about our liberties or freedoms. All he and his "advisers" care about is maintaining global domination to secure their obscene wealth.

If you think I'm paranoid, consider this: Global-1 already owns *all the food in the world.*

No kidding.

The entire world! All the food!

Way back in the 1990s, biotech companies began splicing different genes into already existing plants. They created some new plants. They changed the flavor, taste, and shape of others. They made some crops drought resistant, or able to repel bugs and immune to weed killers. They called these new plants GMOs — genetically modified organisms. They took out patents on everything they created, which meant they owned these new creations.

Oh, and they did one other very interesting thing: They created seeds that don't regenerate new crops. These were called "terminator seeds." For centuries, farmers had been growing new plants from the seeds they got for free from their harvest. But their crops weren't as bright, big, and high yielding as the biotech crops. If they wanted to compete, they needed biotech seeds — seeds that they had to buy new every year. And eventually those biotech seeds mixed with the other seeds, so the biotech companies began to claim ownership of those, too.

During this time, a company owned by Global-1 began to quietly buy up all the smaller biotech corporations. Now there is only one biotech company in the entire world, AgroGlobal.

Face it: Any group that controls the world's food controls the world.

AgroGlobal owns all the food. If they decide not to sell seed to a certain group or nation, they can do that. Any group who defies AgroGlobal can last just one growing season before they begin to starve.

They control you, too. They know everything about you — where you've been, what you've bought, what your doctor prescribed for you, what books and magazines you read. And more. Much more.

Global-1 knows. They invented the tattoo and introduced it in Europe, then Asia, now here. When you get the bar code tattooed on your wrist, you might as well be a plant, because you're about to be gobbled up by Global-1.

The Bar Code Can Be Useful
By Mfumbe Taylor

Read Your Bible
By Nedra Harris

In the King James version of the Bible, Revelation 13:16–18 warns about the Antichrist and his evil plan:

> And he causeth all, both small and great, rich and poor, free and bond, to receive a mark in their right hand, or in their foreheads: And that no man might buy or sell, save he that had the mark, or the name of the beast, or the number of his name. Here is wisdom. Let him that hath understand-

ing count the number of the beast: for it is the number of a man; and his number is Six hundred threescore and six.

The three limit posts that are in lined bar codes correspond to the numbers 6-6-6. They are the three limit posts that guide the scanner. The two at the edges are named guard bars and the central one is the central pattern. Special studies have shown that these three limit posts indeed show the image of 666.

And here's something else to think about — the bar code tattoo was first introduced in the United Federation of Europe by Global-1, on June 16, 2016 — 6-16-16 or 61616. Think carefully before you get tattooed.

Decode Now — Support Dave Young!
By Zekeal Morrelle

Is there a way to fight the tyranny of the bar code, or is it hopeless? It's <u>not</u> hopeless, and there <u>is</u> a way.

Join Senator David Young, the junior senator from Massachusetts, in his Decode Campaign. Join now!

Decode is a group working to defy the tyranny of the bar code tattoo. They propose a set of new laws that will guarantee us the right to privacy: The Young Amendments.

Our society used credit cards and, now, e-cards. All our movements and purchases have been tracked by these codes for so long that we don't even care anymore. But with the bar code we're being expected to <u>wear</u> all our information on our bodies. At least back a few years ago, there was some choice. Until 2020, you could still pay with cash. There were token lanes on the highways (and although there still are, who knows how long that will last? The transit authority — run by Global-1 — is campaigning hard to eliminate them). At one time you could choose <u>not</u> to have a credit card. Your medical records were still between you and your doctor.

Much about you could be discovered through a credit card or e-card, it's true. But with the bar code, our last shreds of privacy are being destroyed. Dave Young is trying to make sure this doesn't happen. Support The Young Amendments. Contact <u>Decode@Senate.gov.</u>

"There's more to this bar code thing than what we talk about in the 'zine," Mfumbe told Kayla after class that afternoon. She'd been on her way to lunch when she saw him standing by the cafeteria door trying to distribute the 'zine.

"What *more* do you think there is?" she asked.

He shook his head. "Not sure. But the articles that come out of Young's office are scary. It's like he's trying to tell us we have to take this really seriously, without coming out and saying exactly why." A student passed by and he thrust the 'zine in front of her. "Decode, now!" he urged her.

She grabbed the 'zine without even looking at him and stuffed it in her bag as she walked on.

Zekeal came alongside them with a stack of the 'zines in his arms. "How's it going?" he asked Mfumbe as he smiled at Kayla.

"Kids aren't exactly lining up for them," Mfumbe reported.

"That's okay," Zekeal assured him. "The movement is just beginning; it'll pick up speed as people become more informed."

Four guys from the varsity football team came out of the cafeteria, laughing and pushing one another playfully. Their bar code tattoos flashed beneath their varsity sweaters as they horsed around. When they caught sight of Zekeal and Mfumbe, their eyes narrowed.

A tall blond guy, Tod Myers, stepped forward. "I thought we told you freaks to put the little magazine away," he said.

Mfumbe thrust a copy toward him. "You might find it interesting. Even if you already have the tattoo, you can choose alternate forms of payment and ID — it's not too late."

Tod and his three teammates formed a semicircle in front of Kayla, Zekeal, and Mfumbe.

"Get lost, we have the right to express our opinions," Zekeal defied them. "This *is* still America. At least the last time I checked."

Kayla folded her arms, unwilling to leave or let them know she was scared. Mfumbe and Zekeal also stood firm.

"Do you have some problem with our government?" Tod demanded.

"I don't have any problem with America," Zekeal replied. "I have a problem with Global-1 and their fascist tactics. It's not the same thing."

"What's the president ever done to you?" Tod challenged.

"Global-1 is cheating me out of the rights I have as an American," Zekeal replied. "They work behind the scenes without letting senators and members of Congress know what's happening. Loudon Waters isn't a president — he's a corporate dictator!"

As Zekeal finished the last word, Tod flung him across the hall, slamming him into the bank of lockers. The football player raised a clenched fist and pulled it back, poised to strike, but Mfumbe leaped onto it.

Two more football players grabbed Mfumbe and threw him into the wall. "Hey!" Kayla shouted. This distracted them for the second required for Mfumbe to slip out of their grasp.

But as Mfumbe jumped back, one of the football players grabbed his shirt and swung him in a wide arc. He hurtled into Kayla, knocking them both across the hall into more lockers. Kayla's face hit the locker vent and her cheek scraped it as she was tugged to the ground by the weight of Mfumbe's hand entangled in her backpack.

A sharp whistle blew and the football players jumped back. Zekeal scrambled to his feet, his forehead bleeding.

"What's going on here?" boomed Mr. Duggan, the science teacher and football coach.

"These guys are disrespecting the United States, sir," Tod reported breathlessly.

Coach Duggan looked at Zekeal. He spotted the 'zines sprawled across the floor and nodded. "Morrelle, what did I tell you about those things?"

"You said they'd make some people mad, but you didn't say we weren't allowed to distribute them," Zekeal answered.

"My guys, all of you, get out of here. And don't let me find you fighting on school grounds again!" Coach Duggan snapped at his players, who hurried down the hall away from them. "Morrelle, Taylor, come with me and bring your papers. You, too, Ms. Reed. Come on."

"We haven't done anything wrong," Kayla insisted. She brushed her hand along her cheek and it came up streaked with blood. "Look what they did to me — to us." Zekeal's right cheek was already a yellow-tinged purple. Mfumbe pressed his left arm to his chest and winced painfully.

"You can see the nurse after you see the principal," Mr. Duggan said.

"Those other guys — your team — they're the ones who should be seeing Mrs. Harmon," Kayla argued.

Coach Duggan was already walking down the hall, leading them to the principal's office. Mrs. Harmon met them in her steel-and-glass office.

"Don't we have the right of free speech?" Zekeal challenged when she told them they could no longer distribute *KnotU2*.

"You have the right to express your political views as you like," she replied in her smooth, unflappable way. "But by distributing your paperwork in the hallways, you are disrupting the flow of student traffic, thereby creating a fire hazard, thereby violating school regulations."

"Oh, come on," Mfumbe scoffed. "You just want to shut us down. Admit it."

Kayla noticed the bar code on Mrs. Harmon's wrist as she continued, "I'll be frank with you. I personally think your cause is 'much ado about nothing,' to quote Shakespeare. Credit cards have tracked our movements now for a half century. Our medical records have long been computerized."

"Yeah, but then you knew who had your information and you had access to it. Now you don't even know what they're saying about you," Zekeal insisted.

"If you have nothing to hide, you have nothing to worry about," Coach Duggan said confidently.

Mrs. Harmon turned to Coach Duggan. "I assume you will speak to your players about our policies regarding fighting in the halls."

"Definitely," he promised, though Kayla doubted he'd say anything to them.

"Now, please leave those papers here in my office before you leave," Mrs. Harmon demanded.

Mfumbe and Zekeal placed their disheveled pile on the principal's desk. She gave them passes and instructed them to go to the nurse.

"It stinks that you lost all your 'zines," Kayla said once they were away from the office.

Zekeal and Mfumbe grinned at each other.

"What?" Kayla asked.

The two of them turned and lifted the backs of their shirts. They'd jammed copies of *KnotU2* into their pant waistbands.

"Final level!" she cheered. Mfumbe and Zekeal held out their hands to her and she slapped them both.

For the first time in a long time, she had a sense she belonged to something.

CHAPTER 5

"Happy birthday to me," Kayla muttered as she opened her eyes on Saturday morning. This was it. Seventeen, the big day.

The phone rang. "Kayla, it's Amber!" her mother called from downstairs.

"I'll be right there," she yelled. With a sigh, she swung out of bed and down the stairs. "Hi, Amber," she said, taking the phone from her mother.

Amber sang a few quick bars of "Happy Birthday to You," then got right to it, as Kayla suspected she would. "Okay, don't thank me. Your papers have been filed by *moi*. You are about to become a code-carrying member of the adult world!"

"You filed a bar code application for me?"

In reply, Amber shrieked, a high-pitched hoot of excitement that made Kayla cringe. "I'll be waiting for you outside my house. Be there at nine sharp."

Kayla hung up and looked at her mother, who sat at the table staring vacantly into her coffee. Her blankness told Kayla that she'd already taken some of the heavy-duty tranquilizer, Propeace, she'd been stealing from the hospital. She'd lose her job if she got caught. But that wasn't the main thing worrying Kayla. Was this zombie the person her mother intended to be from now on? Did she plan to live the rest of her life on Propeace?

"What's up for you today?" Mrs. Reed asked as she continued staring into her cup.

"It's my birthday," she said.

Mrs. Reed glanced up, her eyebrows raised with a rare show of interest. "Oh. Happy birthday. Sixteen, right?"

"Seventeen."

"Whoops," Kayla's mom said with a dull, embarrassed laugh. "Time flies."

"Yeah," Kayla said.

Back in her bedroom, Kayla examined the delicate blue veins at her wrist. She picked a titanium nail file from her dresser and scratched in a bar code, digging deeply into her skin. A dot of blood blossomed out of a vein, making her cringe. How could such a small wound hurt so much? She clutched her wrist, pressing on the veins.

She'd seen a girl in school who had an attempted-suicide scar across her wrists. The bar code tattoo reminded her of that scar. It was practically in the same spot.

Why couldn't she just get the bar code and not worry about it? Mrs. Harmon had called it "much ado about nothing." Was she really making too much of it?

Images of Zekeal and Mfumbe appeared in her mind. They were so confident they were right.

What if they weren't right, though? Maybe the bar code was just a great method of organizing things, proposed by some efficiency expert. Everything was about efficiency these days. It might be obnoxious, but that didn't necessarily mean there was some sinister plot behind it.

Putting her palms on either side of her head, she shut her eyes and squeezed, as if to push down all these maddening, confusing thoughts. When she opened her eyes again, she took in the things in her room as if seeing them as a stranger might, wondering what they might tell someone about the girl who lived there.

Her open closet was packed sloppily with clothing — she had never been neat — last season's silvers behind this year's neon-colored fabrics. Then there was the poster of Ty Zambor, Lunar Tick's drummer, that Amber had given her and even hung for her. The top of her Lucite dresser was strewn with colored sketching pencils, makeup, her handheld organizer, and her pocket-sized communo-disc, the two-inch card that connected her to phones, computers, faxes, and scanners. How much longer would her mother be able to pay the monthly fee on that?

Her eyes traveled to the mirror above her dresser and it reflected back a picture of her father. Startled, she sat bolt upright. No! It was only her own reflection that she'd seen.

What a strange trick of shadow and desire, making her think, just for an instant, that she saw her father in the mirror. She stood and stared at her reflection. Why hadn't she ever noticed before how much she looked like him? The same hazel eyes and wide mouth.

Well, sure, everyone always said she looked like her grandmother, her father's mother. It made sense that her father looked like his mother as well. She had often wished she'd known Grandma Cathy better, but she'd lived so far away and died ten years ago. It was funny not to know someone from whom you'd inherited so many of the genes that made you . . . you.

Digital numbers streamed from pole to pole of her clock. *8:45. 8:46. 8:47.* Titanium wires that carried them were nearly invisible, making the numbers appear to float in midair.

Amber would be waiting for her. She had to decide.

Out in the hall, her mother shuffled by and, in a low voice, sang a song from the early days of the century, the days when she had been a young woman. "*I'm like a bird, I only fly away. . . .*" The bedroom door swung shut behind her.

Kayla pulled on her hot-pink, stretch one-piece suit and finished the look with black boots. She grabbed her silver solar jacket from the closet and snapped out the wrinkles before she slid into it.

Checking her image in the mirror, she put on silver lipstick and black eyeliner.

That's good, she approved her look.

No sad songs for her. No suicide. No beatings in the school hall. She would fit in, go along, and be okay. Life was too difficult to do it any other way.

In ten minutes she was out of the house, heading toward Amber, who waited in her tidy, well-clipped front yard and waved when she saw Kayla. "Final level!" her friend cheered. "You have not looked so hot since . . . well, you know . . . your dad and all. Never mind. Seventeen is going to be the beginning of the new Kayla. I just know it."

"Thanks."

"Promise me you'll dress like this on Monday at school. You'll have the guys dragging their tongues along the hall after you."

"Ew!" Kayla laughed at the bizarre image.

"You know what I mean, Kayla."

What would Kayla say to Mfumbe and Zekeal when she showed up with the tattoo on Monday? She admired Mfumbe and liked him. She wanted him to like her. And Zekeal . . . she couldn't stop thinking about him. She tried so hard not to because Nedra was always pressed up next to him. There was no chance anything could happen between them as long as Nedra and he were so tight.

Still . . . Zekeal's face might pop into her mind at any time, even when she didn't want it to. No matter how hard she tried to banish the picture, she was powerless over it.

But she couldn't let him make this decision for her. She had no respect for girls who let their crushes rule their lives. "Come on. Let's go do this thing," she said to Amber, her voice quavering.

They were about to leave when Amber's parents burst out of the front door. Mrs. Thorn was crying while Mr. Thorn stormed angrily toward his sleek silver lite-engine Jaguar.

"What's the matter?" Kayla asked Amber as Mrs. Thorn trailed tearfully after her husband.

Amber rolled her eyes. "You don't even want to know. They've been at it all morning. It's about that new house, the one across town that we were supposed to buy."

Kayla nodded. "The one with the thermal indoor pool and the Virtual Reality Holograph deck in the rec room? Yeah, I remember. I can't wait to try it out."

"Well, you might have to wait a while because something's gone wrong with the deal. Mom's flipping because our house is already sold and she doesn't know if they'll be able to get into the new one."

"What went wrong?" Kayla asked.

"Something's screwy with Dad's bar code. The mortgage company rejected him when he applied for the mortgage. They scanned it and suddenly the deal was off. This morning they just got the news that a second bank turned him down, too."

"But your dad has a good job," Kayla said. Amber's family had always been better off than Kayla's. They weren't exactly rich, but Amber usually got whatever she wanted.

"I know he does. That's what's so weird. They tried Mom's bar code but something's up with that, too. The people are due to move into our house next week. My parents tried to put them off, but they insist on moving in."

"Where will you live?"

Amber shrugged. "I guess we'll go to a motel or maybe get a room in the new skycomplex outside town." Mr. Thorn's car screeched out of the driveway and onto the street. At the top of the drive, Mrs. Thorn buried her face in her hands and cried.

"Should you go see if she's okay?" Kayla asked.

Amber stood a minute, shifting from foot to foot, uncertain what to do. "She'll be all right," she decided. "Mom gets hysterical, but she always calms down."

They headed for the post office at the center of the transbusiness district. It would take about ten minutes to get there on foot. Even though mail was no longer delivered there, everyone still called it the post office.

As they walked, Kayla wondered what the scanner had picked up in the Thorns' bar codes. What secret had the bank uncovered? She glanced side-long at Amber. Was it something Amber knew and wasn't telling? Or was she as clueless as Kayla had been about her own father's secret troubles?

Amber wasn't the type to keep a secret, especially from her best friend. She'd tell if she knew. Had Mr. and Mrs. Thorn known there was something in their bar codes that could hurt them, or had it come as a huge surprise? Would there be a surprise like that lurking in her bar code as well? She couldn't imagine what surprise could be possible. Bad computer grades? Did that sort of thing show up?

The line outside the post office was only about six people long when they arrived. The sky had clouded. A cold rain began to fall.

"This crashes!" Amber griped, clutching her thin lime-green sweater tightly.

"Let's go home," Kayla suggested. An uncomfortable pressure had formed just outside her consciousness, an uneasiness. Maybe it was just her uncertainty about the bar code, maybe only the grimness of the day.

"Don't worry," Amber assured her. "The line moves fast. Hey, did your neighbor ever tell you his big top-secret info about the 'too?"

Kayla shook her head. "I haven't seen him."

"He's avoiding you because there *is* no top-secret info."

"Maybe," Kayla agreed.

Small flecks of hail began to fall. The sharp, tiny ice bounced from the ledge of the window just over her head, clicking rapidly. The icy rocks sparkled against the glass. Kayla watched as they bounced in every direction. Sparkling . . . sparkling . . .

*　　*　　*

They move slowly toward the city along with the other people streaming toward it. Something is droning in her ear. A mosquito? No, a fighter jet. It streaks low over the crowd. Sleek and impossibly low. Too low. Her companion clutches her wrist. Something explodes. A blinding ball of fire. Flat on the ground, her face in the dirt, searing heat above her.

*　　*　　*

Her eyes snapped open. The line had moved quickly and she'd somehow moved along with it. They were only three people away from the door. She grabbed Amber's arm. "I don't want to do this. I can't," she said, her voice nearly a sob. "We have to go. Please! Now!"

In a moment she would run, with or without Amber.

Kayla tugged on Amber's arms, trying to yank her from the line. Her friend resisted and smiled at the others on line. "She's just really banged out about this whole thing," she explained, embarrassed. Amber placed her hands on Kayla's shoulders to calm her. "Don't worry. Everyone does this now. It's no big deal."

"I'm not kidding! I'm leaving!" Kayla tore free of Amber's grip. She darted out into the road, zigzagging through the cars. Amber came after, calling. Kayla turned to her —

A gunshot from inside the post office cracked the quiet.

Amber stopped, frozen.

A second shot.

Three of them.

A pause. Then a fourth.

The last shot blasted through the post office window. Blood sprayed up from inside, streaking the glass.

This morning, postal worker Gene Drake, 28, was lethally gunned down by Global-1 security guards who opened fire after Mr. Drake destroyed equipment and threatened customers in the Putnam Central Post Office. Mr. Drake was employed at the post office, where he had recently begun administering the bar code tattoo. His actions were apparently an attempt to close down the post office and curtail any further coding.

Screaming loudly, Mr. Drake ripped the bar-coding laser machine from its mount on the desk and hurled it into the wall. He then made death threats toward the people inside and reached for his pocket. At this point, security guards who had come out from the back room deemed Mr. Drake a serious threat to all present and opened fire.

Before joining the post office in late 2024, Mr. Drake had been employed as a tattoo artist at Vincent's Tattoos, across from the GlobalTrac bullet train station in Peekskill. Globalofficers' records show that Mr. Drake was given the opportunity to join the post office rather than serve time in prison for illegal tattooing. Drake's co-workers described him as pleasant to work with, though they claim he had become increasingly withdrawn in recent weeks.

One witness to the scene, Susan Gilardi, 17, of nearby Mt. Kisco, said she was next on line when Drake suddenly demanded that she and the others on line drop to the floor. She says Drake began to scream, "I am an artist, not a cattle brander." He then turned to the people on the floor and told them they'd be better off dead than tattooed.

Mr. Drake rented a house with two other postal employees, who are currently wanted for questioning in the matter of some Global-1 stolen computer passwords that Mr. Drake had in his possession at the time of the incident.

CHAPTER 6

Red police globes lit the street below Kayla's bedroom. She sat in the window of the dark room, not wanting to attract any attention. All the lights were on next door and she could see the police ransacking the rooms. In front, Gene's two roommates were led out in handcuffs.

She pictured Gene, his nervous blink, the unstable way he'd shouted at his dog, his Chinese cigarettes. He was definitely tightly wrapped . . . but there had also been something she liked about him, something friendly. What had spun him over the edge?

Turning from the window, she went to her bed and wrapped herself tightly in her quilt. The red lights still swirled around her dark room.

Trembling, Kayla began to cry. She sobbed for the loss of her father, and now for Gene. Her tears were filled with loneliness, frustration, and fear. It felt like they might never stop.

A week later, Kayla climbed the metal stairs to the second floor of the Route Nine Motor Inn where Amber and her parents were now living. Amber stepped out onto the metal walkway in front of her room. "Hey," she said with a weak smile when she saw Kayla.

"Hey," Kayla returned the greeting. They leaned their arms against the railing and watched the traffic pass. It was almost night, with the last bit of lavender light streaking across the dark sky.

"How did it go?" Amber asked.

"Nothing," Kayla reported. She had been on a job search that day. Her mother had lost her position at the hospital two weeks ago — the same day as Kayla's birthday and the shooting. Since then, money had been very tight. It turned out that her parents had no savings. When her mother's last e-deposit was spent, all their money would be gone.

"Since I don't have the bar code, I'm crashed," she told Amber. "No one wants to even talk to me if they can't do an ID check."

"Just get the stupid tattoo," Amber advised.

"How can you say that after everything that's happened to you and your family? Your parents' bar codes have something so banged out in them that even hotels won't take you guys!"

"Tell me about it!" Amber laughed scornfully. "This place is such a dump they don't even *have* a scanner. That's the only reason they let us in. My parents paid with Mom's mink. Next week her Rolex platinum watch is going. It's costing us thousands to stay in the creepiest hole in town."

"Don't you want to know why this is happening?" Kayla asked. "Obviously it has something to do with the bar code."

"Of course I want to know!" Amber exploded. "Do you think I like this? Dad has called everyone to try to find out why his bar code is such a bust. And guess what now."

"What?"

"He's probably going to lose his job. A guy at work passed him the word."

"That's horrible! What will you do then?"

Amber jerked her head toward her father's Jaguar and her mother's SUV parked down in the lot. "Everything we own except our furniture is jammed into those cars. I guess we can keep trading it until the stuff runs out. My cousin invited us to come stay with her, but no one wants to go. She's a member of some new religion that doesn't believe in fun."

"No fun?" Kayla asked.

Amber nodded. "No music, no makeup, no downloaded programming, even."

"You're kidding," Kayla said.

"I wish I was kidding." They watched more cars go by before talking again. "But, you know, Kayla, some people are doing great with the tattoo. You might be one of them. I just read a thing in the paper today. They're talking about bringing in kids over seventeen if they see them out at night without a bar code. They charge you for not having proper ID."

"They keep saying they're *going* to do that, but they don't really do it," Kayla disagreed. "They can't. There's no law that says you have to get a bar code. It would be illegal for them to just haul you in."

"Kayla, I don't know why you're being so stubborn about this," Amber cried. "You *need* the 'too. Face it!"

"The shooting at the post office — it was like . . . like a warning," she argued.

"It was just a freaky thing that happened!" Amber said. "Lucky for us that you left when you did. We were standing right by that window. We might be dead right now, if you hadn't taken off. But we're not. We're alive, and being alive means you need a bar code."

"Why did Gene Drake get all banged out over the bar code? Why did he say the people in line would be better off dead?" Kayla challenged.

"I don't know! Because he was crazy!"

"But maybe he knew something about the bar code that *drove* him crazy. Like . . . like . . . my dad."

"Sorry. I didn't mean to say your dad was crazy. That wasn't what I meant."

Kayla looked away from Amber. "It's okay. I suppose it's possible that he was mentally ill. He did kill himself, after all. And I think my Grandma Cathy died in some kind of mental ward. No one talks about it."

"Would your mother know about it?" Amber asked.

"She might," Kayla admitted. "But lately she's either drunk or tranquilized or both. It's hard to talk to her."

Angry shouting erupted from inside the hotel room. "We are not living with that old freak!" Mrs. Thorn shouted.

"Fine, maybe you'd rather starve," Mr. Thorn yelled back. "Jake told me my job is on the line."

"You're not losing your job. You're getting paranoid!" Mrs. Thorn replied. A door slammed and there was silence. Then they could hear the sound of Mrs. Thorn sobbing.

"They fight all the time now," Amber told her. "God, I hope we don't have to go stay with my cousin Emily. She's from the planet Bizarre. Besides that, she lives in Nevada."

Kayla locked her hand around Amber's wrist. "Nevada! That's too far away. I'll never see you again. No, you can't go. You could live with me."

"What would your mother have to say about that?" Amber asked.

"My mother wouldn't even notice that you were there!" Kayla assured her with scornful laughter. "Half the time she doesn't know *I'm* there."

"That's too bad," Amber said softly, "because I always liked your mother. I thought she was nice, you know."

Mrs. Thorn came out onto the walkway, her

eyes red-rimmed. "Amber, your father and I need to speak to you about something." She noticed Kayla and nodded. "Sorry, family emergency."

Kayla once again job hunted on the way home from school the next day. No one seemed too enthused about employing a girl without a bar code.

"It's not just the bar code itself," the manager of a diner told her in a smooth, confident tone. "It's what it represents, what it tells us about the kind of person you are."

"Obedient, compliant," Kayla offered. She meant to be sarcastic, but her irony was obviously lost on the manager, who smiled and nodded.

"Exactly," the woman agreed. "A get-along kind of team player — that's the kind of gal we're looking for. Come back and see us when you get your tattoo."

While sitting on the bulletbus, heading home, Kayla thought of one more place where she could apply for work. She got off the bulletbus at a stop in front of Artie's Art, a scruffy store where she usually bought her art supplies, and went inside. "What can I do for you, kiddo?" asked a skinny man with a shaved head.

"Could you use some extra help, Artie?" she asked. "I need a job and you know I'm here all the time, anyway, so you'd barely have to train me."

"Got a 'too I could scan?" he asked.

Her heartbeat sped up, but she fought to seem casual. "No — I don't believe in them."

He stared hard at her for a long moment. "I'll give you eighteen an hour."

"That's minimum wage!" she objected.

"It *would have been* minimum wage if they hadn't done away with it last year," Artie corrected her. "And one *reason* they did away with it was so small-business types like me could hire teenagers like you — ones without bar codes — for cheap. Twenty-two dollars an hour, but you have to go outside and hand out flyers when we're slow."

Kayla stretched her arm across the counter to shake. "Deal!" she agreed excitedly. As they shook, she saw that he didn't have a bar code, either.

Kayla calculated her earnings all the way home. Though it wouldn't be much, it meant she and her mother could eat.

At her front door she took out her keys, but the door swung open when she touched it. They always locked the doors when they came and went. Something was wrong.

Cautiously, she stepped into the front entryway to the living room. Some kind of motor was running. No. Snoring. It was snoring.

Following the sound, she found her mother passed out on the sofa, her left arm dangling off the side. Her bar-coded wrist had been rubbed raw. A nearly empty bottle of vodka sat on the low table beside the couch.

Kayla dropped into the easy chair across from the couch. At least the snoring told Kayla her mother hadn't overdosed on Propeace and vodka. Not yet, anyway.

"Hey, Mom, I got a job," she spoke bitterly to the sleeping figure. "Isn't that great! Yeah. I knew you'd be excited."

Entering the kitchen, she found an egg in the refrigerator and scrambled it. There was no bread for toast. Fortunately, a box of saltines had been pushed to the back of a cabinet and been overlooked. Saltines and eggs — egg, actually — wasn't a bad dinner. As she ate, she surveyed the messy kitchen and considered cleaning it.

The phone rang. "Hello?"

On the other end, someone emitted an anguished sob.

"Amber? Is that you? Amber? What's wrong?"

CHAPTER 7

The Thorns were stuffing the last of their belongings into the SUV when Kayla got there. Amber ran to meet her as she walked from the bulletbus stop into the parking lot. "Dad got fired. We're leaving!"

"Did you ask if you could come live with me?" Kayla asked.

Amber nodded tearfully. "I asked but they said no. Like, really no. My mother's not speaking to me. She's mad that I even asked. I know it hurt her feelings but I can't stand this. I can't leave you and school and all."

"I got a job today," Kayla told her.

Amber wiped her eyes. "That's great."

"Maybe we could find a place together. I mean, I'd have to give my mother some money, but we could find some little dump down by the river. We'd be okay."

Amber pressed her forehead on Kayla's shoulder as sobs shook her body. "I have to go with them," she spoke through her tears. "They need me or they're not going anywhere."

"What do you mean?"

Amber held out her wrist. "This is the only bar code that works at the gas pump."

"Are you kidding?" Kayla cried. "Don't they have e-cards?"

"They didn't work when they tried them," Amber replied. "My code works, though. Dad had his last e-deposit sent into my account. Mom dumped all her accounts into it, too." She laughed miserably. "Hey, they'd better be nice to me. I have all their money."

"This is so banged out!"

"You don't even know! You haven't met my cousin Emily." Amber spoke in gasps. "She belongs to this really strict religious group. It will be so horrible."

Kayla remembered Nedra's piece in *KnotU2*. "Some people think the bar code is the mark of the devil. Does she have one?"

Amber looked up at her. "Oh, she's got one. And it works just fine. I guess her beliefs don't include worrying about that."

Mrs. Thorn stood by the SUV. She was crying just as hard as Amber. Mr. Thorn washed the windshield of his Jaguar, his face a blank.

"*I'll* ask if you can stay," Kayla pleaded.

Amber wiped her tears with her sleeve as she shook her head. "Don't bother. They'll just tell you we're a family and we have to stick together."

Kayla rubbed Amber's back. "It'll be okay." She didn't know if it would be okay or not. Somehow she doubted it, but what else was there to say?

Both of the Thorns' cars started up at once. "Amber, come on," her dad called.

Amber threw her arms around Kayla and squeezed tight. "This isn't happening. This isn't happening," she murmured.

"Amber!" her father shouted again, this time with an edge of annoyance in his voice.

Amber let go and her face was soaked and red. Her nose and eyes were swollen from crying.

"Send me your new web address. I'll e-mail you all the time," Kayla promised.

Amber nodded, then ran across the parking lot and climbed into the front seat of her father's car. Kayla waved as the cars pulled out.

It would be a long drive to Nevada. Kayla had never been west. Amber might as well be relocating to the station on the moon.

When they were out of sight, Kayla stood another moment, feeling a hole rip open inside her. This afternoon she'd had a best friend. And now Amber was gone.

How had all this happened to them? The Thorns' lives were ruined. Her own family's, too. Her father dead, her mother completely messed up. She'd gone from having a family to feeling completely alone in the world.

This awful loneliness was new to her. At first she didn't even recognize it for what it was. She only knew it as a gnawing ache in the pit of her stomach. As she stood there, though, the ache transformed into an overwhelming fear, the feeling that she was vulnerable to some unknown danger and there was no one to help her. She had no one to turn to and she wasn't enough on her own, wasn't strong or smart enough for all the challenges.

Although she was on a busy roadway, Kayla felt completely alone. It was the last thing she wanted to feel. She needed to be around people, even if they weren't people who cared about her. But where?

A car pulled up to the light on the road behind her. Loud rock music blasted from inside. As the light changed and they drove off, she saw them veer up a side road going toward the warehouse district down by the river, near the nuclear reactors, where the hottest clubs in the area were.

The city bulletbus pulled to its stop half a block away. On impulse, she dashed for it, using her school pass to pay the fare. Fifteen minutes later, she got off at the GlobalTrac station down by the river.

She began walking along the river, which was turning orange in the setting sun. It wound down to the warehouse district.

Geese flew overhead, returning for the spring. The old song her mother had been singing came into her head, the part about not knowing where her soul was.

What was a soul, anyway? People talked about the soul all the time, but she had no idea what they meant.

It was almost dark by the time she reached the warehouse district. The lights of the nuclear reactors illuminated the whole area, but the warehouses below them didn't emit any light. They were mostly windowless and had no identifying signs. You had to know where you were going in order to get there.

Kids at school said that the warehouses contained clubs that ran all night, even though the local law said clubs had to shut down at twelve. There were rumors about guns and the newest drugs being available down here. She wasn't looking for trouble, though — just to be around people.

She'd heard of one club called Lobo2MeClub. Kids at school went there because there was supposedly no bar code check at the door. It was easy to get in if you were under seventeen and could make yourself look old enough.

With no idea where the club was, Kayla moved through the dark pathways winding through the square brick buildings. Occasionally, a door opened and someone swung out, an explosion of blasting rock music hitting the street for a moment and then shutting down as the door closed again.

Kayla intended to ask for directions but the people all exited too quickly into waiting cabs or cars. She kept walking until she reached a very dark end of the cement pathway. Even the lights from the reactors didn't shine here.

Another cluster of dark warehouses was just ahead. As she walked, she became aware of footsteps behind her. Glancing behind, she saw a male figure in a dark jacket.

She quickened her pace.

He began walking faster, too.

She didn't want him to know she was scared, but she could sense the distance between them closing. Her legs began to run, seemingly without waiting for her mental command.

He ran, too. His footsteps pounded behind her. If she screamed, there was no one there to hear.

In seconds he'd be upon her.

CHAPTER 8

A hand clamped onto her shoulder.

She swung around, hoping to land a smashing blow onto his nose.

He blocked her swing, gripping her wrist. "Whoa!" he cried. "Hold on!"

"Zekeal!"

His voice was a rasp. "I couldn't call you. I'm losing my voice."

She covered her hammering heart with her hand and bent forward. Nausea came in a wave, then passed. She had never been that terrified before.

"Sorry I scared you," he said. "I saw you turn down here and came to get you. There aren't any clubs in this section and it isn't exactly safe. What are you doing here?"

"Do you know where the Lobo2MeClub is?" she asked.

"The Lobotomy? Yeah. You meeting someone there?"

She shook her head. "Just needed to get out."

"That's where I'm going."

"Really?"

"It's where I'm going now," he replied. "Come on."

She followed him back out of the darkness and he yanked open a black metal door at the first building they came to. Blasting music assaulted them as they walked in. It was so loud, it vibrated in her skull.

It was *exactly* what she wanted.

He pulled her close when a slow song came on. It was as though electricity ran between their two bodies. She wouldn't have been surprised to see a snapping white current running up their sides.

In that wordless exchange they'd made a connection. "It's hot in here," he said, still moving to the music. "Let's go upstairs to the roof."

A different song came on. She'd heard it for the first time just that morning on the radio. "Okay," she answered. "But first I want to hear this."

"The Monsters," he noted. "They're astral." He wrapped his arm around her shoulders and again she felt covered in that invisible veil of energy.

The Monsters
"Quasimodo"
Written by Kurt Conklin
(Music pounding)
I am a freak. I walk this planet. I don't know my name.

My thoughts are melting into puddles. Some

days I am insane. I cannot say what's in my heart or what I think in my brain. I am a freak walking the planet in constant pain.

(Softly)

But your love puts me away. Your love puts me away.

Is it real? Is it real? Is it real?

Is it a dream? Is it a dream? Is it a dream?

Your love puts me away. Your love puts me away.

With you it's all okay. With you it's all okay.

(Pounding)

I am a freak and there is always ringing in my ears.

My head is pounding with a million terrifying fears.

I do not know if I can last another day or if I can even remember how to pray. I have one thought and that is for you to stay. Esmeralda, stay. With you it's all okay.

CHAPTER 9

"I know how the guy feels," Zekeal said softly.

"You do?" Kayla questioned. He didn't show that kind of hurt. No one would ever guess. He always seemed completely self-assured.

"Sometimes," he admitted. "Let's go upstairs."

She followed him through a back door onto dark hallway stairs. They came out to the roof of the club. The lights from the reactors were nearly blinding. Slowly, her eyes adjusted.

He leaned against a waist-high wall running the perimeter of the roof. Taking hold of her wrist, he gently drew her closer to him. Turning her hand palm up, he ran his finger along the delicate blue veins of her hand, tracing a line down to her wrist.

She looked out at the river, which reflected the lights from the generators on its black surface.

"I heard about your dad," he said. "I'm sorry."

"Thanks."

"Do you have any idea what . . . drove him to it?" he asked gently.

"My mother says the bar code killed him, but I'm not sure why she says that. It banged him out, though. He went into this deep depression right after he got it."

She read pain in his large, dark eyes. *He understands how it is*, she realized. *The bar code's affected him, too.*

"My dad got fired and my mother kept getting promoted in her job after they were tattoed," he said. "At first, they both worked for a biotech lab. Dad burned out of every job he had, kept getting fired. Mom started thinking of him as a real loser. They fought about money all the time. Pretty soon they broke up."

Another family wrecked by the bar code. "That's banged out," Kayla said. "Which one of them do you live with?"

"It got so I couldn't stand either one of them, so I just cut out. The place I have now is a real dump, but at least it's quiet. My parents aren't there screaming at each other day and night."

"That must be hard for you," she said, "being all on your own."

He grinned, though no light came to his eyes. "I get a little hungry sometimes."

"I know what you mean," she said with a bitter laugh, remembering her own often-empty refrigerator. "Good thing my dad prepaid my cafeteria fee at the beginning of the year or some days I wouldn't get any food at all. God, the beginning of the year feels like it was a long time ago. In September, the bar code didn't seem like a big deal. I didn't think it would have any effect on my life."

"That's because we've all gotten used to being tracked through the Internet. It really started in the 1970s when credit cards were first linked to computers," he said. "By the 1990s somebody knew every move you made with that card."

"If this has been going on for over thirty-five years, why does the tattoo seem so horrible? And why is it turning people's lives upside down?" she asked.

"There's something more in that code," Zekeal said, his eyes narrowing thoughtfully. She got the idea from his quick reply that this was a question he'd considered many times before.

"What do you think it is?" she asked.

"I wish I knew. I feel like there's a missing piece to this puzzle. Once we know what it is, a lot of things will make sense." His eyes brightened with an idea. "Listen, when I met you tonight I wasn't really coming here. I was going to a meeting. Come with me."

She hesitated. What kind of meeting? It didn't really matter, though. There was no way she would willingly part from him. They'd connected and she needed someone to be connected to, especially an attractive, exciting somebody like Zekeal. "Okay."

She followed him out of the club and back to the dark end of the warehouse section, where she'd met up with him that night. They walked quickly to the last warehouse; she jogged at times to keep up with him.

Nothing more than black woods stood beyond that last low warehouse. Even the reactors' lights weren't pointed in that direction, leaving the area in shadow. Zekeal pulled hard on the metal door. When they stepped inside, Kayla folded her arms against the cold air.

"Where have you been?" an annoyed voice demanded. "And what's *she* doing here?"

Kayla turned toward the voice and spied a circle of light at the far end of the darkness. Four figures sat around the light.

Zekeal took Kayla's hand and, again, his touch ran through her like a jolt of electric current. He led her through the black middle area toward the group. "I'm here now," he replied calmly.

"This is a *secret* meeting," the same voice reminded him reproachfully. Kayla was close enough to recognize the four figures — Mfumbe, Allyson, August, and Nedra. Nedra was the sharp-voiced one, obviously angered by Kayla's presence. When they were in the lighted circle thrown by a bare-bulb lamp set on the floor, Zekeal took hold of Kayla's wrist and pushed up her sleeve, presenting it to the group. "She's okay. Seventeen. Not coded."

Mfumbe smiled at her. "Final level," he said with an approving grin. It was good to see him there. She was always calmed by his friendliness. From the very first day they'd met, she'd felt comfortable with him.

Nedra, August, and Allyson eyed her warily.

"Where did she come from?" Nedra asked.

"I ran into her and saw she had no bar code," Zekeal replied. "I say she stays."

"I guess she's okay, then," August said.

Nedra grunted and stared down at Kayla's chunky-heeled black boots. Kayla felt a wave of guilt. Nedra was right not to like her, to be suspicious, but not because of the bar code. She *would* take Zekeal from Nedra if it were possible. She wouldn't do it to hurt Nedra. She just simply wouldn't be able to turn him away if he came to her.

Zekeal disappeared into the darkness outside the circle and returned with two folding chairs, one for Kayla and one for him. They sat as August opened his handheld computer. The monitor up-lit his round face. "Okay, what are we working on for this issue?" he asked the group.

Allyson spoke first. "I want to do an article on cloning."

"What's that got to do with anything?" Nedra snapped.

"In Europe they don't have the same bans on cloning that we have here," Allyson explained. "Some of the first human clones are now turning seventeen and are being refused bar codes."

"Global-1 probably wants to get patents on them," Nedra sneered. "They have patents on every-thing else, on human organs, on genes, on chromo-somes — why not patent clones? If you looked on the butts of those kids, you'd probably find the Global-1 trademark stamped there."

"Probably," August said with a laugh. "But they're still people; I wonder why they can't get the bar code."

"Nobody in the government is saying," Mfumbe said. "The parents of the cloned kids are raising a stink about it. They say that not having a bar code makes kids outcasts."

"That's exactly what *we're* saying!" Zekeal shouted, getting up and starting to pace. "Soon no one will be able to do *anything* without the bar code. Anyone who hasn't got it will be shut out of everything — just like in Europe."

"Soon?" Nedra scoffed. "It's already happened."

"I agree. My friend Amber just had to move," Kayla joined in. "Her parents *have* bar codes but there's something in their codes that's messing up their entire lives."

"They have no idea what it is?" August asked.

Kayla shook her head. "None."

"Stuff like that is happening all over the place," Mfumbe said. "Everything's getting turned around. But, you know, in some cases it's all good. My dad used to feel like he couldn't get a break at work. But since he got his bar code, he jumped right over his boss's head for a promotion. Now he's his old boss's boss. For him, getting the bar code has been great."

"Nice for *him*," Zekeal grumbled. Kayla was sure he was thinking of his own father. She thought of her family and Amber's. She remembered Gene Drake and his housemates. If the bar code was good for the Taylor family, she was glad — but then why was Mfumbe fighting it?

"Why are you here?" she asked him.

He shrugged. "Principle, I guess. Even though it's worked out for my father, I don't like it. And it's humiliating to be branded like that. It makes me think of the German concentration camps."

Kayla admired that he was able to think of more than himself. It took intelligence and moral strength, she thought, to act on principle instead of simple self-interest. Not many people could do that. It made her like him even more.

"I don't trust it, either," Mfumbe went on. "I don't want to put something permanent on my body before I know what it's all about. I don't think they're telling us everything there is."

"What else could there be?" Kayla asked. She thought there was something more to it, too. But what?

"We don't know," Mfumbe answered. "But the government is too determined to get everybody tattooed. I just know there's something more."

He's got to be right, she thought. All her instincts told her that he was. A mere e-card, license, and medical record couldn't be messing up lives like this, could they?

"You're paranoid," Nedra said. "It could easily screw you up if they saw you had too many traffic tickets, or bad credit. That would be enough to mess things around if you applied for a job or wanted to buy a house. You don't need any hidden thing."

"I suppose," Mfumbe gave in. "It just seems to me that there *is* something else in there."

"Allyson, I'm giving you three columns on the front page for your article on cloning," August told her. "Is that enough?"

"Should be," Allyson agreed. Kayla noticed that she held a black box about the size of a small nuclear oven on her lap.

Zekeal told August he needed at least four columns to write about how Senator Young was hoping to block a bill in the Senate that would make the bar code required for anyone receiving public assistance. "They say that people on welfare should be required to make it easy for the government to identify them," he told them. "As if people should lose their civil liberties because they're poor."

Kayla hoped her job at Artie's Art Supply would pay enough to keep them off public assistance. It was strange to imagine her mother and herself being on welfare. They'd always been so . . . middle class.

Mfumbe asked for space to do another political cartoon. "I have a comic strip in mind that shows people having to marry someone that the bar code picks out for them."

"That's not so far-fetched," Allyson said. "For centuries, people have married mates within their own social class. Now the bar code is creating new social classes."

Mfumbe scribbled something on his pad, then began to sketch. From the way he kept looking up at her, Kayla suspected he was sketching her portrait.

Finally, Nedra secured her space for an article on the history of the bar code. "Let's see what the websites are doing," August said, tapping away at the small computer keys.

"I want to see what Dave Young's up to," Zekeal requested.

"That Dave Young is just a rich guy with a cause," Nedra sneered.

"That's exactly why he's our best bet," Zekeal replied. "Rich guys are the only ones who can get anything done. His father is Ambrose Young, the head of the Domestic Affairs Committee in the Senate."

"Yeah, but Ambrose Young isn't like his son," August mentioned, still typing. "Didn't you hear that report yesterday? They found out that Young senior has a ton of stock in Global-1." He hit two more keys. "I'm in."

They huddled around the handheld monitor and read. Several links brought them to different related sites. There was a petition in favor of maintaining at least one codeless lane on all highways. Another site enabled you to order preprinted cards for sending to senators to protest the mandatory bar coding for public assistance bill.

After that, they checked anti–tattoo code websites from around the country. Kayla had never dreamed there was such a massive resistance movement. It was encouraging and it meant she wasn't so unique in her concern about this. She wasn't a paranoid malcontent. There were even lawyers who agreed with this group and insisted that the bar code was a total violation of civil liberties.

"Hey, we're in time for a chat on the Dave Young site," Zekeal remembered. "Let me type." August gave him the laptop. Mfumbe sat beside him so that he could type, too.

DY: This is important stuff. If we let Global-1 push their bills through unchallenged, I predict we will find ourselves living in a dictatorship that will rival anything Orwell ever concocted.

MT: Are you talking about the book *1984* by George Orwell?

DY: Yes. I suggest that you all read it if you haven't already. Avoiding that kind of world is what's at stake.

ZM: What can we do?

DY: Stay on top of information on upcoming laws and proposals. Contact government officials. Let them know how you feel.

ZM: Don't you think we have to do something more radical?

DY: Not yet. If we can head this thing off at the start, I hope we can avoid a lot of problems later.

"That's vague," Zekeal mumbled. Mfumbe typed.

MT: If the bar code becomes required, would you advocate civil resistance to it?
DY: That's why we're working so hard now — so it doesn't come to that.
MT: But if it did happen, would you suggest that all people resist and not get coded, on the grounds that it is an unconstitutional law?
DY: Can't say right now.

Zekeal clicked them out of the chat room. "What did you do that for?" Mfumbe protested.

"He's avoiding the issue," Zekeal said, standing. "Dave Young's a great guy, but that avoidance thing crashes me."

August clicked them into a website in San Francisco. The anti-code group on that site was claiming that the bar code linked you to the devil. She remembered Nedra's article with the quote from the Bible.

August clicked out of that site. "That group thinks drinking milk links you to the devil."

"Don't laugh," Nedra snapped. "Maybe it does. AgroGlobal owns every dairy farm on earth and all their cows are transgenic, which means they've been altered to produce more milk. As far as I'm concerned, Global-1 *is* the devil."

"Who's ready for this?" Allyson asked, tapping the case she held.

"I am," Nedra said quickly.

Allyson opened the case and slid out a small metal piece that looked like a computer mouse with a monitor in it. She held it up to her eye and clicked a button.

"What is that?" Kayla whispered to Zekeal.

"A virtual reality headset," he told her. "Allyson's father has no idea she takes it out. She had to sneak to load her eye scan into the lock just so we could unlock the case. She's such a genius, she was able to do it."

"What do you use it for?" Kayla asked.

"You'll see," Zekeal said.

CHAPTER 10

August lifted the virtual reality helmet off his head. "Your turn," he said, handing it to Kayla.

"All right," she agreed. "What's going to happen when I turn it on?"

He turned a dial. "I set it to take you to the next resistance frequency we can pick up. They change depending on who's sending. But basically you should have the sensation that you're inside a resistance website."

"Where did you just go?" Zekeal asked August.

"I was attending a meeting of resisters in Canada. They were all talking French. I had no idea what they were saying." He laughed. "It was kind of final level, anyway. They were all so excited."

Kayla glanced at Mfumbe for reassurance. Her eyes asked him if she should try it, and he nodded. She placed the helmet on her head.

August told her what buttons to press and soon the helmet was humming on her head. The vibration ran down along behind her ears and traveled through her jaw. She shut her eyes as the sensation continued down the back of her neck.

Lights filled the blackness behind her eyes and

formed blobs that crossed and blended into new colors. Sometimes they separated, reminding her of the films she'd seen in science depicting cell division.

She began trembling as the vibration from the helmet overtook her whole body.

Then, somehow, she was on a rock outcropping on a mountain. Below stretched a mountain range so vast and far-reaching that it seemed to go on forever, until it faded into ethereal blue. Somehow she'd lost the helmet.

To her right, a woman with long black hair sat beside a small fire. She wore a cowboy hat that boasted a wide band of gorgeous feathers, as well as jeans and a heavy woolen poncho. She held a bundle of grasses and herbs that she waved over the fire, sending out plumes of white smoke and a pleasing herbal smell. With eyes tightly shut, she chanted a wild, poignant call that seemed to emanate from the center of her being.

Kayla stepped closer. The sound of her footfall on the gravel-strewn rock caused the woman to slowly open her eyes. She fixed on Kayla but betrayed no emotion.

Kayla felt awkward under the scrutiny of such an unwavering gaze, but only a little. A larger part of her was too fascinated with this situation and this person to be overly self-conscious.

The woman beckoned and Kayla sat across the

fire from her. "I've felt you calling me, so I called to you," the woman said in a smooth, deep voice.

"I . . . called you?" Kayla questioned. What was she talking about? She didn't even know who this was.

"My name is Eutonah. You want to know about the soul."

Kayla breathed in sharply. "How did you know that?" she asked.

"We're all part of the same dream. Those who know how to listen can hear," Eutonah replied. "The soul is the original being — what the being was before it entered the earthly plane, what it will be again when the earthly plane is done with."

Kayla felt as if she were in a dream. It was the same as a dream, where something made no sense and yet seemed perfectly logical at the same time. "How do you know it's there?" she asked. "The soul, I mean. There's no proof it even exists."

"You are your soul. There is no *it* other than you."

"Where am I?"

"Remember this place," Eutonah said. "Imprint it in your mind's eye so that your internal guidance will enable you to find it again when you need to. Remember the white face." Getting up, she walked off down a dirt trail until she disappeared into a pine forest.

The icy wind blew up the back of Kayla's shirt

and she shivered again. The wind blew so hard and cold that she squeezed her eyes shut . . .

. . . and was back in the warehouse, the helmet on her head. "Where did I go?" she asked, lifting it from her head. "I met an amazing woman. I was in the mountains somewhere."

August took the helmet from her and examined its readout. Mfumbe looked on with him. "I never saw these numbers before," August said.

"*What* numbers?" Kayla asked.

"The numbers on the helmet tell what virtual reality site you've been at. It sounds like you traveled to the Adirondack Mountains. A lot of resistance groups live around there," Zekeal told her.

The Adirondacks? Kayla remembered that her father had maps of the Adirondacks at the time he died. Her mother had thought he was planning a vacation. "Why would resisters go to the Adirondacks?" she asked.

"It's easy to hide up in the mountains," Mfumbe explained, "and they're close to Canada. If things really went bad, you could get into Canada inside a day. Canada doesn't have the bar code yet."

"Yeah, but these numbers are new. It's a site we've never been to before," August said. He looked to Kayla. "What exactly did you see?"

She described the location and the woman.

"I've heard about Eutonah. She's a Cherokee shaman and a bar code resister." Allyson said. "She was putting out articles warning against the bar code when the thing was still in Asia. There's a mystical angle to everything she writes. The article I read was about how you can resist the bar code with your mind."

"How do you do that?" Nedra asked, clearly skeptical.

"Well, according to Eutonah, we all have un-developed telepathic and telekinetic powers," Allyson said. "She claims we can all learn to access those abilities."

"So what are we supposed to do, float the bar codes off everyone's wrist with our brain waves?" Nedra scoffed.

Allyson stayed cool. "She says the power of our minds is so powerful it's atomic. And it's true. We're atoms. That's what we're made of."

Kayla closed her eyes and imagined Gene Drake deflecting the guards' bullets with the power of his mind. If only he'd been able to. Then maybe he could have closed down the post office and they would have brought in reporters. Then he'd have told the world what he knew about the bar code.

"That's just nuts." Nedra spat out the words. "I don't believe you even saw her, Kayla. You probably just read an article and dreamed up the whole thing to get attention."

"That's not true. She was real," Kayla insisted. "She told me to remember the white face. Does that mean anything to any of you?"

They glanced one to the other, then shook their heads. "No," said August, "but maybe we *should* remember it, just in case we need to know it later on."

"That's crazy. She didn't see anybody," Nedra insisted.

"How do *you* know Kayla didn't meet her?" Mfumbe argued with Nedra. "The Adirondacks is resistance central. Some of those groups are nutty, walking around the woods with machine guns, or trying to contact passing spaceships. But it's the center of everything. If you need to know something about the bar code resistance, eventually you have to touch base in the Adirondacks."

"You know," August said, "now that you mention the Adirondacks . . . I want to talk to you guys about something. I mean . . . I *don't* want to talk about this, because I hope this doesn't happen, but I think we have to. . . ." He breathed deeply, as if to steady his nerves. "What if this all starts to go down badly? It could, you know."

"What do you mean?" Zekeal asked.

"Say Dave Young can't make a difference and Global-1, or the government or whoever, starts coming after resisters," August said.

"I don't think that will happen," Allyson replied.

"Okay . . . I hope you're right, but if it does, I think we should have a plan," August said. "Someone to contact or someplace to meet."

"What about the Adirondacks?" Mfumbe suggested. "It would be a good place. You could follow the Superlink straight up. Eventually you'd run into other people who would be sympathetic to you. It wouldn't be too hard to find help."

"If it's so easy, then Global-1 could find you, too," Nedra pointed out.

"The Adirondacks are huge," Zekeal said. "They wouldn't find you that easily. But, for the same reason, we'd never find each other. We've got to have a specific spot."

Kayla thought about the place where she'd just been. Eutonah had said she'd need to find it. Would she someday meet this group there? Was her future already that intertwined with theirs?

"I'll get some maps," August volunteered, "and then we can pick a place to meet."

"August," Allyson said abruptly. "Is there any more space available in the 'zine?"

He opened his 'zine files and checked. "I could probably piece together a column or so. Why?"

"When I was using the helmet, I got into a San Francisco website where they were discussing Tattoo Gen," she said.

"I've heard of that," Mfumbe said. "What did they say about it?"

"What is it?" Kayla asked.

"It's a gung-ho youth group funded by Global-1," Allyson explained. "They're very into the bar code — a tattoo pride kind of thing."

"That's sick," Zekeal said.

"It might be sick, but it's real. The San Francisco group was saying that they're very open in the Bay Area," Allyson reported. "They wear these bar code T-shirts and highlight their tattoos in fluorescent colors. Lately, gangs of them have been wearing a red jumpsuit uniform and beating up anyone who's not coded."

"Is anyone doing anything to stop them?" Mfumbe asked.

"If they are, I haven't heard about it. They said that here in the east, Tattoo Gen is much more undercover. They have a mission to seduce kids into getting the bar code. If they see someone who's undecided, they befriend them and try to talk the person into it."

"That's so low," Kayla said.

Allyson nodded. "I'd like to write an article in the 'zine exposing the group."

"No one will believe you," Nedra argued. "I'm not sure if I even believe you. I've never seen one of them."

Allyson sighed, exasperated. "That's the point, Nedra. You're not *supposed* to see them. They're undercover — at least on the East Coast."

"I don't believe it," Nedra insisted.

"I can give you the space if you want it," August told Allyson.

"I want it," Allyson agreed as she placed the helmet back into the case.

Zekeal stood. "I've got to get home. If I don't write that report for science, I'm not graduating."

"Me, too," Mfumbe agreed, folding his chair. The glowing light from the bare bulb guided them out of the warehouse until August shut it off with a remote clicker from the door.

Mfumbe locked the heavy door and afterward showed Kayla the metal key. "Can you believe people depended on these once?" he said. "This door is one of the last of its kind. It's so primitive."

Kayla studied the key he handed to her. "Where did you get this?"

"My dad owns this warehouse," he told her. "He inherited it from his father. I think he's forgotten all about it. I just took this key from his desk one day when I was a kid and I've been coming down here ever since."

The group walked together past the clubs. Nedra headed for a sleek silver sports car. "Are you coming, Zeke?" she asked.

Zekeal looked trapped, shifting from foot to foot. "Yeah, sure," he said with a quick wave to Kayla.

Nedra tossed a triumphant glance at Kayla before slipping into the car. Behind her, August and Allyson got into August's beat-up 2010 magnetic Honda, one of the first of its kind ever made.

"I can drop you off," Mfumbe offered.

"Thanks, but I'll walk. I don't live far." She wanted to walk along the river and think about everything — to brood about Zekeal jumping into the car with Nedra after all. How could she have so totally misread the situation?

"You sure?" Mfumbe checked.

She nodded. "Yeah. Thanks."

He was nice, really nice, and she suddenly had the feeling that he might be interested in her, probably had been for a while now. He was attractive, too, with those striking light eyes against his dark skin. But it was Zekeal who made her heart race, who had gotten into her head. All she wanted now was time alone to replay the evening they'd spent together.

She walked back toward the river. The nuclear power plant lit her path for a long time, until its glare faded and gave way to the softer light of the full moon. As she went she relived the jolt of energy she'd felt as he'd turned her palm over, checking for the bar code. She went over everything: the vulnerable expression on his face when he'd talked about his family, the adrenaline-charged half second when she'd turned and seen he was the one who'd been following her, his calm command when he'd insisted she be allowed to stay at the meeting.

The bulletbus took nearly a half hour to come to its stop at the GlobalTrac station. By the time it let her off, she felt she'd been away from home for a long time — even though it had been only hours. So much had happened.

As she neared her house, she saw a figure by the halogen lamppost in front. The intense glow of the white light made him easy to see.

She hurried toward Zekeal, knowing exactly why he'd come — for her. He'd come for her.

He saw her running and walked quickly toward her. When they met, he held her and kissed her hard.

NEW PHENOMENON OF SELF-IMMOLATION PUZZLES PSYCHIATRISTS

Baltimore, MD. May 15, 2025 — A team of psychiatrists at Johns Hopkins Medical Center held a press conference today describing a bizarre new medical phenomenon they've dubbed Tattoo Manic Psychosis. Dr. Herbert Carver, head of the team, described this mania in which a person becomes convinced that the bar code tattoo will somehow do him or her harm. This creates a state of deep disturbance within the person.

The first stage of TMP (Tattoo Manic Psychosis) is often manifested in self-destructive behavior such as alcohol or drug abuse. At stage two, the person becomes desperate to have the bar code removed at any cost, despite the fact that bar code tattoo removal was outlawed in the same 2024 bill in which tattooing for decorative purposes was also outlawed. The patient can become so desperate to have the bar code removed that he or she resorts to an attempt to burn the bar code from his or her skin. "This has resulted in many catastrophic burns," Dr. Carver told the press. "In the last six months we have treated nearly 200 people for self-inflicted immolation."

May 17, 2025
To: Artgirl@globalnet.planet
From: (AT)cybercafe1700@globalnet.planet

Hey, Kayla,

I finally got to a cyber café in Carson City. I'm here with my cousin Emily to buy stuff. She and I are the only ones who can actually make a purchase since we have working bar codes. I feel like a secret agent since I have two secret missions.

My first mission is to sneak away and e-mail you. Emily doesn't even have a computer. A few months ago, she decided the CIA was spying on her through the computer, so she smashed it with an ax. Yes, that's right — my cousin Emily is a full-blown mental case! You can imagine what a joy it is to live with her and be dependent on her for everything.

Actually, my code can still buy some things as long as my parents keep my account up. They do this by trading in all their stuff. My dad got lots of credits by giving a car dealer his Jag. (Although he says the guy ripped him off big-time because he knew we were stuck.) My code seems to only go so far, though. We tried to apply for a loan for me and it crashed out. It seems like I have the family bum code, too — it just hasn't totally caught up with me yet. I can still get gum and milk and antiperspirant and stuff like that, thank God. As long as they still take it at the gas tanks, we're not totally banged out.

My other secret mission is to buy my mom hair dye. Emily doesn't believe in hair dye. She says people are meant to age naturally, so she won't buy any for Mom. I know it's dumb, but Mom is completely twisted out over this. Every time she looks in the mirror, she gets all teary. So I said I'd try to score her a box while I'm in town. I don't know how Mom will explain her sudden lack of gray hair. Hopefully, she'll think of something.

Life here is more or less hell. All the kids around where my cousin Emily lives go to Cyber School since there are so few of them; it's not worth building a real school. Since we have no computer and our nearest neighbor is miles away, I can't even do that.

Well, enough about the horrendous waste of my young and beautiful life — how are you? I'm going to stay here in the café for as long as I can and hope you get this message in time to reply.

Amber

May 17, 2025
Reply to: (AT)cybercafe1700@globalnet.planet
From: Artgirl@globalnet.planet

Amber! I can't believe it's you! I am <u>so</u> glad (shocked, amazed, thrilled) to hear from you. I'm sorry your cousin Emily is so banged out. But don't feel alone. Everything is weird here, too. You wouldn't recognize Winfrey High, at least not the teachers. They made them take this big test and then dumped the ones they claimed didn't do well. I don't believe it, though. Mr. Curtin, our Language Arts teacher, is one of the best teachers in the school. Well, he's one of the teachers who didn't pass the "test." The other day I saw him collecting cans on the road for recycling. He had a big plastic bag full. I wanted to talk to him, but I thought it might embarrass him to have one of his students see him. But I noticed one thing about him — he doesn't have a bar code. And get this! Mr. Kerr — my guidance counselor — he's now the principal! We have these big assemblies every week where we explore our "feelings." Aghh!

So much bizarre stuff is happening. My neighbors, the Ferns, disappeared one day. The Globalofficers came to our house asking if we knew where they went. My mother was friendly with Mrs. Fern, but she had no idea that they were planning to leave. (Although that's not really so odd. She's completely clueless about most things these days.)

Actually, you're not the only one who has secret missions, either. I've started having a secret love affair with Zekeal Morrelle! Here's why it's secret: Nedra Harris and Zekeal used to go with each other and he's afraid that she'll go ballistic and try to make trouble for one or both of us if he doesn't break off with her just right. So we're waiting for June, once school is out and they all graduate, for him to tell her. That way she'll go away to Cape Cod for the summer with her family, like she does every summer, and we won't ever have to see her again.

Because of this, we're not openly seeing each other, but I go to his place a lot at night and we find time to be together whenever we can. I'm just so completely in love with him. And I know he feels the same.

Are you still there? Can you reply?

Kayla

May 17, 2025
To: Artgirl@globalnet.planet
From: (AT)cybercafe1700@globalnet.planet

Oh, thank God you're there. I'd have died if I missed you. Don't get mad. I'm only saying this because I care about you, but what's with Zekeal Morrelle? Do you really think Nedra H. is such a flaming psycho that he can't break off with her? Are you sure he isn't two-timing you? I don't want you to get hurt. And, yes —

he's gorgeous. But what good is gorgeous if he turns out to be a creep?

Sounds like your mother isn't doing too well. ☹ How are you two living? Tell all!

Amber

May 17, 2025
Reply to: (AT)cybercafe1700@globalnet.planet
From: Artgirl@globalnet.planet

My job at Artie's has been great. I love working for Artie, and it's the only thing paying the bills.

I'm not mad at you for what you said about Zekeal. I'm also worried that he's handing me a line about Nedra, but I don't really think that's what's happening. I can't believe he ever liked her. He says he thought she was "hot."

The KnotU2 group has become my whole life. August, Allyson, Mfumbe, and, of course, Zekeal have become like a family to me. (Does that make Nedra my evil stepmother?)

Damn. Mom just came in the kitchen door. She's stumbling all arou . . . she fell.

G2G, K.

CHAPTER 11

"Sorry I'm late," Kayla said, slipping into the empty chair they'd left for her. She didn't feel like explaining how getting her drunken mother settled on the living room couch had made her late for the meeting.

Mfumbe smiled at her with his eyes, then leaned forward into the circle. "Someone should do something in the next 'zine on that article that just came out about TMP," Mfumbe suggested.

"Tattoo Mania Psychosis?" Allyson recalled.

Mfumbe laughed scornfully. "Yeah, can you believe they made up a disease to explain why people are so banged out by their bar codes that they try to burn them off? They don't mention that these poor people didn't start out completely detonated — the bar code has driven them crazy."

"I'll write that article," Allyson volunteered. "Okay, so everyone has an assignment for the next issue. We're done."

Kayla caught Zekeal's eye and, for a second, they were together. Then he broke the connection by turning to Allyson. "Kayla needs to use the helmet," he reminded her.

"I just put it away," she complained. "I mean, if you want to, Kayla, I'll —"

"That's okay," Kayla told her. "I'll get it next time." She and Allyson were becoming friends, in a way. They were very different, but she admired the girl's brilliant mind and calm manner. "It's my fault for being late."

"You didn't miss too much," Mfumbe said. "We did 'zine assignments and then we tried the virtual reality, but there were mostly just warnings about Tattoo Gen from resistance groups."

"They claim the group is growing fast in the Northeast," Allyson added. "I'll take their word for it, but I haven't run into them."

"Me, neither," Nedra said. "I don't believe it."

"Why would they make it up? Be careful who you talk to," Mfumbe advised. "Whatever you do, don't tell anyone about this warehouse."

"As if anyone *would* talk to us anymore," Allyson said with a bitter laugh.

Kayla knew what she meant. She had become increasingly unpopular at school for being against the tattoo. Just yesterday a girl's foot had shot out and hooked itself around her ankle while she was descending the stairs. Kayla had saved herself by grabbing on to the side railing. The girl hadn't even stopped or apologized.

"I guess we're done," Zekeal said to the group after a moment of dead air among them. At that cue they headed for the door.

"Hey, Allyson, I heard about the scholarship," Mfumbe said as he locked the warehouse door.

"That's really final level. It was the genetics article you wrote that aced it, wasn't it?"

Allyson nodded. "Genetics has changed the world," she said. "Everything is genetics."

Kayla knew what genes did, although she still wasn't totally clear on what they were. She knew they made you what you are, no matter if you were a person or a plant. She knew that cloning occurred when genes reproduced without sex, creating an exact copy of themselves. In school, there was endless debate over whether people were completely controlled by their genes or if their environment affected human development more than genes did. It was an intensified version of the nature versus nurture debate.

They began walking toward their cars, past the clubs. "Did you know that we have almost the same genes as flies?" Allyson said. "Yet even though our genes are nearly the same, we're people, not flies. Why? Why does that happen? It's so mysterious and, even after all these years, no one knows why this is. I want to work in biogenetics at Harvard and get my Ph.D. in it."

"Why did you say genetics has changed the world?" Kayla asked her.

"Geneticists can already predict who will get certain sicknesses and who won't," Allyson replied. "They know this information even before birth. Insurance companies could save millions of dollars by refusing to insure those people whose genetic code is less than final level. People at high risk for cancer and heart disease could be identified and rejected right away."

"They could also be identified and cured," Mfumbe said.

"You're always an unrealistic idealist," Nedra said to him.

"He's got a point," Allyson said. "It all depends on how the science is used. That's why the field is so vast. I mean, what happens with genetics and cloning is all up to the people who are doing the work."

"And guys like Dave Young who are passing the legislation," Zekeal added.

"They affect what happens in *America*," Nedra said pointedly. "They can pass all the laws they want in America, but everything is worldwide now. They can just go to another country and do whatever they want. Remember their name — *Global*."

"Dave Young knows all that," Zekeal said. "He's working on all kinds of international trade bills to protect Americans."

"You and your Dave Young," Nedra snapped at him. "I'm sick of hearing about him like he's some kind of god."

"He's not a god," Zekeal came back at her angrily. "But right now he's the best hope any of us has of not becoming slaves of Global-1."

"They already own us," Nedra shot back.

"If you think that, why don't you get the bar code?" Allyson asked.

"I don't know," Nedra admitted. "Maybe I know they own us all and I'm just mad as hell about it. Maybe I just like banging my head against a wall, for the fun of it."

For a moment they all looked at her. Was she right? Kayla experienced a profound feeling that she was. It flooded her with sadness, the sense that all freedom and true human dignity were things of the past, that the future held nothing but restriction and conformity. Art that came from computer-generated images, as well as life that came from computer-generated acceptance. What if all they were doing was acting out their anger at inheriting a world that held nothing truly good, really nourishing for any of them?

"They don't own us," Kayla said softly. "Not yet, not if we fight them." She hadn't planned to say that, wasn't even aware that she truly believed it. But the words had come from somewhere inside her and they were hers.

"Kayla, do you have anything you want to write about in the next 'zine?" August asked.

The offer startled her because they'd never invited her to do anything for the 'zine before. She'd accepted this because they were older, and also because they were all so brilliant in their own way. Without admitting it to herself, she'd assumed she wasn't equal to any of them — not in brains, courage, or even in the ability to express herself. Her first impulse was to claim she had nothing to say, but there *was* an idea that had been forming in her mind.

"I think so," she answered cautiously. "I want to do an article pointing out how everything around us is changing, all our lives. Why is the bar code turning our lives around?"

BAR CODE TATTOO
NOW REQUIRED BY LAW

In a stunning surprise vote the Senate approved President Loudon Waters's bill requiring all citizens to be tattooed with their personal bar code on their 17th birthday

---

Washington, DC. May 19, 2025 — By a slim margin of four votes, the Senate approved President Waters's proposed legislation requiring all Americans aged 17 and above to acquire the bar code tattoo originally sponsored by the president's Global-1 party. The tattoo has been used widely in Asia and United Europe since 2006. It has been required in China and Japan since 2010, and in the Federation of United Europe since 2012. Speaking from the Rose Garden this morning, the President stated that this step will keep the United States current with international fiscal policy and make international banking a more fluid process.

Senator David Young, the junior senator from Massachusetts, lodged an official protest and called for a revote. Senator Young spearheads a protest group called Decode. The group's objective has been to ensure that an alternative to the bar code is always offered in every transaction. "This alternative method of payment and identification guarantees Americans the freedom of not being tracked by any organization," said Senator Young. "This is an essential right under the Constitution. It is a critical part of what separates free Americans from those living under repressive regimes around the world. Freedoms such as this must be protected at all cost."

Senator Young is the son of Senator Ambrose Young of New York, who just last month retired as head of the Domestic Affairs Committee. Mr. Young senior said that his son had "many valid points to make in his opposition to the mandatory enforcement of the bar code tattoo."

Senator Gary Gill of Mississippi told the press that Young's Decode organization was comprised of nothing more than young people searching for something to rebel against and the criminal element looking to hide their "unsavory past."

CHAPTER 12

Kayla stood in the doorway studying her mother, who sat in front of the computer in the den. She'd gotten so much older looking in such a short time. The open file on the monitor in front of her read: *Joseph Reed, Department of Human Resources, FBI.* Silently, Kayla stepped into the room behind her and began to read. The file contained statistics on her father: *Five foot eleven, brown hair, size eleven shoe.*

"This is Dad's FBI file. How did you get into it?" she asked.

Mrs. Reed jumped. She hadn't heard Kayla come in. "Someone e-mailed me the password to open this. The person just signed it 'A Friend.' I tried to reply, but the message came back saying the sender was not a known address."

"So? What's in there?" Not waiting for an answer, Kayla kept reading. The file named her father's blood type, his cholesterol level, his standing heart rate, his bone density.

Then came another bar code. It was different from the first bar code at the top of the screen. Which was the bar code that had appeared on his wrist? And why were there two of them?

A series of coded letters and numbers appeared

beneath the second bar code. Slowly Kayla realized — based on graphs she'd seen in her science textbook — that the second code was a gene sequence; a series of genes appearing next to one another, represented as a bar code.

In science this fall they'd studied how geneticists used a bar code to show a sequence of genes. The number-alphabet codes beneath listed individual genes.

Kayla continued reading.

Advantages:
IQ 115
genes found for: heightened powers of logic; visual acuity; above-average spatial relations; color sensitivity; creativity; fit musculature; longevity.
Questionable/Possessing both positive and negative aspects:
genes found for: empathy; mental psychic tendency; low levels of extrasensory perception.
Liabilities:
genes found for: alcoholism; iconoclastic tendencies; delusional, hallucinatory schizophrenia.

Kayla looked at her mother. "Dad didn't drink and he wasn't schizophrenic," she said.

A bitter smile spread across her mother's face. "Knowing what I already know — it should have been plain."

"What?" Kayla shouted. "What do you know?"

Mrs. Reed grabbed Kayla's wrist. "Good. You haven't gotten that damned tattoo. No matter what you do, don't let them make you get it."

"It's the law, Mom. Haven't you heard? I could be arrested now for not having a bar code!"

"I don't care," her mother replied passionately.

"Why? Mom, please tell me what you know," Kayla pleaded.

Her mother got up from her desk chair and walked to the window. "No. I can't. It's better if you don't know."

Kayla grabbed her mother's arm. "How can it be better?"

"I can't talk about this!" Mrs. Reed said angrily. Hurrying to the front door, she went out, barefoot, into the rainy evening.

The computer screen blacked out. White letters appeared on the screen: ACCESS DENIED.

Kayla sprang to the door. "Mom!" she called. "Come back!" She ran down the front walkway after her, but her mother had gone out the front gate and was walking quickly down the street.

Tears came to Kayla's eyes . . . but what was the use of crying? Her mother was no help to her anymore — she might as well just accept that. Ashley Reed was in a world all her own, haunted by private demons Kayla might never know about.

"Anything I can do?" A familiar voice made her turn. Zekeal was beside her. Obviously, he'd come from the other side of the street and had seen some of this humiliating scene.

"Hi. Why are you here?" she said, quickly wiping her eyes.

"I don't have your number. I came to tell you we're having an emergency meeting. You heard the news today, right?"

"Yeah."

"Want to hang out at my place until the meeting at six?"

"Can't. I have to work."

"I'll walk you there."

"What about Nedra? Someone might see us together."

"We're just *walking* together," he said with a shrug. "I'm getting sick of this."

"Tell her about us, then."

He looked past her, thinking. "It's less than a month now. It will be easier to just let her fade away."

"Easier for you," Kayla said. "Not easier for me."

"I'm sure she knows something's up. You're right. I'll tell her tonight."

"Really?"

"Yes. After the meeting."

"Come inside with me," she said. "I want you to see something." Taking his hand, she led him into the house and brought him to the computer.

ACCESS DENIED still floated on the screen's black

background. "Do you have any idea how to get back into that file?"

"What is it?" he asked.

"My father's FBI file."

He looked at her wide-eyed. "Decode thinks that may be the database used by the bar code. You actually saw it?"

She nodded. "Everything about him was in there."

He sat down and began punching the keyboard. "I'm a pretty fair hacker," he said. "Let me have a crack at this."

Kayla had the file on her mind as she walked across the parking lot to Artie's Art Supply an hour later. Zekeal had gotten in, but for only a minute. It was long enough, though, for him to see the file. "That's it," he had said. "This is the big secret, the thing they don't want us to know."

"The genetic code?" she guessed.

"Absolutely," he agreed. "Your whole genetic code is in there. They know everything about you. Everything."

She rattled the glass door to Artie's. The sign on the front door read CLOSED. The store was dark although she always worked on Thursdays at four. "Artie!" she shouted, banging on the glass. "It's me! Open up!"

Artie, his wife, and their two kids lived on the second floor. Walking around back and up the steps to the porch on the second floor, she peered in the window. The furniture was still there, but the apartment was dark.

In the distance a siren screamed and Kayla tucked her fingers around the end of her jacket sleeve, hiding her wrist. Where was Artie? Why hadn't he opened the store?

Kayla walked back to the street and got on a bulletbus headed for Zekeal's apartment down in Peekskill. Zekeal lived in a run-down apartment near the GlobalTrac station. Now boarded shut, Victor's Tattoo Parlor had once operated on the bottom floor.

Kayla climbed the wooden back stairs and banged on the door. "It's open," he shouted.

She stepped inside and found him sitting in the one main room at a table in front of his large, old-style computer. Instead of looking at the screen, he was reading a thick book, a manual. He looked up at her and grinned. "Hey! I thought you were working," he said.

"Artie's was closed. I don't know why," she explained.

"That's weird," he replied, turning toward her in his seat.

"What are you reading?" she asked. Without waiting for his reply, she flipped the open book to its cover.

TATTOO GENERATION:
A MANUAL OF PRIDE

She questioned him with her eyes.

"A friend got this to me so I could see what we're up against," he explained. "It's banged-out stuff. These people are totally convinced that the bar code is the way to an exciting new future."

Kayla opened to the middle of the manual and scanned the page.

You influence by example, of course. Proudly sporting your tattoo is the best assurance that it will gain prestige in the eyes of the undecided. But direct influence is also an effective way to persuade your family and friends that there is nothing to fear from the tattoo. The resistant person will often have an unwarranted suspicion of direct persuasion. That is why it is best to take an indirect approach. Do not reveal your mission, but rather — in a friendly way — point out the futility of remaining untattooed. Those who can neither buy nor sell face a future of certain failure. By pointing this out, you plant the seeds of productive thought among those resistant to the tattoo. Also, point out that going against the wishes of the United States Senate is unpatriotic. It is every citizen's duty to comply with the wishes of its government. Complying is not only patriotic, it's also an attractive trait. The untattooed person risks social ostracism. He or she openly demonstrates that he or she is not a team player.

This will be enough to persuade most people that remaining untattooed is a liability they do not wish to incur. Special operatives may be permitted to remain untattooed for the express purpose of winning the confidence of the uncoded. Their records will remain on file at Tattoo Generation headquarters for a period of no more than one year. After that time, the agent is expected to become tattooed and carry on his or her duties as an exemplar of bar-coded life.

Kayla looked up at Zekeal. "This is scary. Why do they care if everyone is tattooed? Can't we all just do what we want?"

Zekeal sighed. "This thing is huge now," he said. "It might be more than we can fight."

Kayla had never heard him speak like this. He was usually so confident. His doubt worried her. Was he giving in? Had this new ruling about a required bar code shaken him that deeply?

"What about Senator Young?" she asked. "You still believe in Decode, don't you?"

Getting up, he slapped the Tattoo Gen manual shut. "Dave Young tried, but look what just happened. It's depressing. And after today, seeing what I saw in your father's file . . . I don't know." Zekeal gently drew her up from her chair. "Let's talk about it over here," he said, leading her to his faded futon couch.

They sat and he pressed his weight against her until she was lying back, beneath him on the futon. She wrapped her arms around his neck and, closing her eyes, let his warm lips press down on hers.

They rolled together there, straining against each other. Outside, the rain came down with a steady beat. A steady beat . . . beat . . . beat . . .

*   *   *

She is outside the white wall. People around her have fallen to the ground, knocked back by the blast. The man with her is very near. She still can't see him clearly. There is smoke in the air. Fighter jets are above them. But no more explosives drop.

"Send it away," the man says to her telepathically. She sees that the people around her are looking up at the jet. Their eyes stare at it, unwavering.

She stares at the jet, too. "Go away. Go away. Go away," she tells its pilot, thinking hard on her message.

The jet turns and disappears behind some clouds.

The people stream toward an opening in the wall. No one speaks, but she hears their cries clearly in her head. "This way. This way into the city. Hurry." She is running, following the others toward the opening in the wall.

*   *   *

He'd stopped moving on top of her. "Kayla. Where are you?" he asked, sounding offended. "You're not here with me."

Opening her eyes, she drank in his beautiful face. "I am here. I am. Really. I'm with you." She pulled him to her and held him close, hoping he would never leave her.

"Don't worry," she said. "I love you."

They had all arrived at the warehouse meeting, except Nedra. For once Kayla was anxious for her to come. Tonight Zekeal would tell Nedra that his relationship with her was over. After the afternoon she had spent with him, Kayla didn't think she could go another minute sharing him with anyone else.

"We'll have to start without her," August said after a ten-minute wait. "We have to completely rethink the next issue of the 'zine. It's got to be much more forceful. And we need to think about what we'll do if things get worse. We're in an emergency now and —"

The warehouse door banged open. Nedra strode across the warehouse. The unfamiliar clack of her footsteps told Kayla that Nedra wore high heels with the straight skirt she had on. Nedra didn't usually dress like this.

As she came into their circle of light, Kayla saw that Nedra's arms and legs were covered up and down with colorful, swirling tattoos. It was impossible to tell if they were permanent or not.

Nedra turned seductively in a circle, displaying her new body art. She sidled up to Zekeal and extended her leg through a slit in the skirt. His name was emblazoned in purple up its side.

He stared at it, then up at Nedra. She smiled coolly back at him.

"What's going on, Nedra?" Allyson asked.

"I wanted you to see the new me," she replied. "The brand-new me," she added, stretching her arms wide.

A hushed gasp ran through the group. A bar code tattoo was clearly visible on her right wrist.

"I don't believe you did that!" Zekeal said to her.

"I'm not getting arrested — not this girl. In fact, I'm out of here. Zekeal, you'd better come with me."

Zekeal got up and walked out with Nedra.

CHAPTER 13

"Well, game over. I never thought Nedra would do *that*," August said.

"Nedra goes where the power is," Mfumbe noted. "She liked Zekeal and she thought we had a shot at winning this, so she came with us. Maybe she was just mad, like she said. Now, though, she thinks Global-1 is unbeatable, so she's shifted her position to their side. Nedra's an extreme person — whatever she does, she does it all the way."

"People who are extreme on one side lots of times become extreme on the other," Allyson pointed out. "We've got to watch out for her now."

"I don't think so," August disagreed.

"You wait and see," Allyson insisted.

Kayla couldn't believe they were so calm. She was reeling from the scene she'd just witnessed. Zekeal had walked out with Nedra — and Nedra just got the bar code.

What did that mean to the group? To her?

"Did Zekeal just walk out on us for good?" Kayla asked them, struggling to keep her voice normal.

"I guess they needed to talk," Allyson suggested. "I'd be surprised if he's gone for good."

"If he listens to her, he's a fool," August said.

"We have to be careful how we handle her," Mfumbe said. "She knows everything about us, and she's not necessarily on our side anymore."

August took a map from his pocket and handed it to Mfumbe. "I've circled Lake Placid. It's a pretty big town in the Adirondacks. We'll all be able to find it."

"Shouldn't we go somewhere more out of the way?" Mfumbe questioned.

August shrugged. "We could meet and then get out of there pretty quick. None of us knows the mountains. I'm not exactly a mountain man. We might get lost."

"That's true," Mfumbe agreed as he scanned the map for Lake Placid.

"Yeah, well . . . in the meantime, I have a pretty big problem I need to tell you guys about," Allyson said. "You know I won that scholarship."

"What about it?" Kayla asked.

"I can't collect the scholarship without the tattoo now."

"Do you *need* the scholarship?" Mfumbe asked. "Your family is pretty well set up, aren't they?"

"Yeah. I need it because my dad's being a real creep about this. He's been wanting me to get the tattoo ever since I turned seventeen last August. He says that if I blow this scholarship, he won't pay for college. He says I think credits grow on trees, blah, blah, blah, and all that. But it doesn't really matter what he says. I can't even get into college without the bar code."

"Let's go online and hopefully some of the resistance websites can give us advice," Mfumbe suggested. He took out his laptop and logged on. His face furrowed into frown lines as he tried to get into the different websites. August looked along with him, also looking worried after a few minutes.

"What's wrong?" Kayla asked.

"This is weird," Mfumbe told her. "None of the sites will open. It keeps saying, *This page currently unavailable.* The only one open is the Dave Young site. Let's wait for Zeke to come back for that one."

Kayla glanced anxiously back at the door. What was going on? Were they finalizing their breakup? Or was Nedra winning him back?

"I bet the sites have shut down because of the new law," Allyson said. "They're afraid they'll get busted. Let's try the headset." She unlocked the case with her eye scan and picked up the helmet. "Who wants to go first?"

August took the helmet from her and put it on. He set some dials and sat with his eyes shut. The rapid movement of his eyes told them that he had arrived somewhere.

Beneath his lids, his eyes darted. Sometimes he frowned, or nodded. After five minutes, his eyes opened and he lifted the helmet from his head.

"I got to the resistance hall in San Francisco, but nobody was there, just a custodian cleaning up the building," he told them.

Mfumbe went next. Like August, his facial changes and active eyes told them he'd reached a destination. Kayla glanced at him from time to time but never took her eyes from the door for long. What was taking so long? He should have been back. She was dying to see Zekeal, to be assured everything was fine.

Mfumbe returned from his virtual experience and reported that the resistance site in Michigan was also empty. "Globalofficers came in," he told them. "For a minute I thought they were going to arrest me or something. Then I remembered that I was really here."

Allyson tried to get to a resistance site in Orlando but also came up with a location without participants. "Is everybody hiding?" Allyson asked. "What's going on?"

Kayla took the helmet from her and set the numbers for Eutonah. Again the vibrations made her whole body tremble.

And then she was there, on an outcropping near the mountaintop. Eutonah sat nearby at her campfire.

She smiled at Kayla. "Come and sit," she said. When Kayla was seated cross-legged on the dirt next to her, she continued, "What I'm about to say now will be important, so listen. The Dark Times that were foretold are being fully expressed. Stay focused on your truth. Move toward love and you will be safe."

Eutonah stretched toward Kayla and kissed her on the center of the forehead. Kayla felt engulfed in the woman's powerful life energy. "You can come to us in time of need," she said. "Remember the white face."

When Kayla reopened her eyes, the fire still burned, but Eutonah was gone. How had she disappeared so soundlessly?

Kayla stared into the dark path beneath the towering pines, the place where Eutonah had probably gone. The trees shimmered in front of her eyes. It was as if they were separating into their molecular elements.

And then she was back in the warehouse.

"Any luck?" Allyson asked her. Kayla told them she'd found Eutonah. "She said 'the Dark Times are here,' or being fully expressed, something like that," Kayla reported. "She also told me to remember the white face. What does that mean?"

The group looked one to the other, then shook their heads. "No idea," August said.

"Listen," Kayla said to the group. "Today Zekeal and I got a look at my father's FBI file. We think it's the file the bar code uses. His genetic code is in his file. Why do you think it's there?"

"It was really there? That's it! I've had the feeling that there's some definite connection between the bar code and genes for a long time now," Allyson said. "Global-1 is lifting all the bans on human cloning at the same time they've made the bar code a requirement. There's got to be a connection."

"You're just obsessed with genes," August said.

"No — I agree with Allyson. I have that feeling, too," Kayla jumped in. "All the genetic information on my father was represented as a bar code."

"I've seen that genetic bar code," Allyson said. "It's a creepy coincidence."

"I've seen it, too," Mfumbe said. "You're right. It's bizarre."

"But what has it got to do with the bar code?" August wondered.

"It's information that no one knew was in there," Kayla said. "But *why* is it in there?"

"Don't know," Mfumbe said.

When they went outside, they found Zekeal sitting on a rock by the edge of some trees. Nedra wasn't with him. Kayla rushed to his side. "What happened?"

"It's over," he said. "Done with."

She began to tremble. "Between us?

"No! Between Nedra and me."

She took his hand, thankful.

*　　*　　*

An open letter to my friends:

I want you to be the first to hear this. Effective tomorrow morning, I have tendered my resignation from the United States Senate. I've done this in protest against the recent legislation making the bar code tattoo required by law.

With all my heart I believe that this bar code branding is wrong. It's dehumanizing, reducing each person to a number. I know we've been headed in this direction for nearly a century now. People have had social security numbers for ages, but that number was created to connect an individual to a social security account, not as an identity tag.

Daily, I see fellow Americans who work hard, and have achieved a certain success, falling down the social and economic ladder for no ascertainable reason. Conversely, I see people rising in society at a sudden and meteoric rate. What information is contained in those bar code lines that is causing this? I challenge President Loudon Waters to stop denying there is some other information stored in the bar code and to come clean with the American people.

I do not overstate the case when I say that the future of all humanity is at stake here. Now that this reprehensible bill has been voted into law, the need to act is more crucial than ever. I will remain available to you on this website and assure you that I will continue to fight as a private citizen.

It is my sincere hope that all of you will stay

informed and fight this insidious threat to our American values whenever and wherever it arises.

With affection and respect,
David Young

"Do you need to get home?" Zekeal asked as
they lay on the futon together later that night.
Kayla was cradled in his arms. "It's late. Will your
mother worry?"

"Depends how banged out she is," Kayla replied
sleepily. It had been a long day and she felt herself
nearly drifting off. "She was pretty crazy when she
walked out of the house, but she was more wired
than looped. She's probably been drinking since
then and passed out by now."

"Was she always like that?" Zekeal asked, running his hand lazily up and down her arm.

"No. She was great until my dad killed himself,"
Kayla recalled. "A little tense maybe, but always
there for me."

That was the last thing she remembered saying
before falling into a dreamless sleep. When she
awoke, she was alone, but heard the sound of the
shower running.

Zekeal's computer was on and the Tattoo Gen
manual was open beside it. The screen displayed a
list of e-mails.

Curious, she went to the table and saw that the
first four e-mails were from Mfumbe, Allyson, and

August, as well as an e-mail she'd sent him earlier in the day. But the second to last message was from Nedra. The last came from *chtg@Tattoogen*.

With a quick glance at the bathroom door, she clicked on the last message.

To: Agent ZM
From: Agent CHTG-Tattoo Generation

Congratulations on your excellent work. Your request to remain uncoded for an additional two months has been granted. Your connection to Decode has yielded valuable information. We appreciate your sending us candidate Harris as a trainee. She is a very promising young agent. We look forward to meeting the next candidate that you spoke about at our last session. We are confident that Ms. Reed will also be an asset to our group. Thank you for your most recent dispatch. Please make contact again at this same time tomorrow as per our usual schedule.

Thanks again for all your fine service to Tattoo Generation,

CHTG

The room spun and Kayla gripped the table to steady herself. Zekeal was a Tattoo Gen agent? He'd sent Nedra to them, and now he planned to sway her to their side as well?

She struggled with a total, dumbfounded lack

of comprehension. The facts as she'd just read them refused to come together and make sense for her. It was as though her mind was unable to work.

Zekeal was a double agent, working for Tattoo Gen while appearing to work with Decode. That was the simple truth that had so brutally assaulted her. It was the truth that there was no turning away from.

Zekeal was a traitor.

He was recruiting members for Tattoo Gen.

A pain gripped her chest and she felt a tightening sensation. She struggled to breathe, swallowing large gulps of air. This couldn't be true, couldn't be real. But it was.

The shower water shut off and Kayla turned to face the bathroom door, while her brain continued to scream at her in disbelief. *He's working for Tattoo Generation. Nedra, too. You're his next candidate. That's all you are to him.*

Zekeal appeared, dripping wet, wrapped in a white towel. He'd never looked more gorgeous, but she felt no attraction to him. His dark eyes darted between the computer and her outraged face.

"I'm your next candidate?" she asked in a voice thick with disdain and incredulity. Her mind was exploding now with rage. How could he betray her so brutally? How could she have been so absolutely, completely fooled?

He approached her, reaching out and speaking

tenderly. "Kayla, I was going to tell you. There's no beating this thing. It's everywhere now. I wanted to win you over to the tattoo side because I care about you. You won't be able to do anything without the code."

Kayla stepped away from him, knocking the chair over behind her. "You lied to me!" she shouted. "And you've been lying to Mfumbe, Allyson, and August. But not to Nedra. The two of you have been in this together all along. Did you even break up with her today?"

"Yes. I mean I told her that you and I've been seeing each other. I was completely honest about it. But she assumed that was just part of my work with Tattoo Gen."

"Is it?" Kayla yelled, wild with fury. "That's what this has been about all along, hasn't it? You just want another body to deliver to your group." She spun toward the door.

He grabbed her as she pulled it open. "You've got the wrong idea. Maybe it started that way, but —"

"Don't lie to me anymore, Zekeal," she raged, tears flooding her eyes. "Just let me go!"

"No! Not until —"

"Let go!" she screamed, yanking free of his grip. Nearly blind with tears, she ran down the back steps.

Lightning flashed overhead, and by the time she arrived at the bulletbus stop, the sky had opened. The ride home was punctuated with ear-shattering thunder and flashes of riveting light.

At points she felt the urge to get off and get lost in the storm, maybe stand in a parking lot and let the lightning come for her.

More than anything, though, she wanted to get home. It was that strong desire — the same one she'd felt the afternoon her father had slit his wrists.

When she got there, her front door was open, banging in the wind.

CHAPTER 14

"Mom?" she called, stepping onto the rain-soaked front carpet. "Mom?"

There were no lights on, but someone was walking around upstairs. Her mother appeared at the top of the dark stairs. "Where have you been, Kayla?" she asked, her words slurred.

"You left the door open. The carpet is soaked," Kayla said.

Mrs. Reed came down the steps and walked to the living room sofa with only a slight stagger. She was obviously drunk, but her eyes burned with an abnormal brightness. Kayla wondered what drug had brought it on.

This was scarier than a drunken stupor or her mother's vacant stares. This expression reminded Kayla of someone who was seeing visions no one else could see, an insane person. "Mom, are you okay?" she asked, not knowing what else to say.

"Guess where I was today," her mother replied.

"I have no idea."

"Of course you don't. I was at my old hospital. And guess what! Those babies won't need bar codes. Want to know why?" she asked.

"Why?" Kayla asked, standing alongside the couch.

Her mother stared up at her, her eyes wide. "Because they're now inserting chips in every baby's foot. And in those chips is each baby's complete genetic code."

"Their genetic code?"

"That's if they live long enough," Mrs. Reed went on. "You see, they blood-test those little babies right away. That blood test tells them which babies will grow up to be healthy and strong, and which ones will have health problems. The ones who aren't healthy are being left to die."

"No!" Kayla gasped. "I don't believe it."

Her mother got up and began to walk in stumbling circles around the room. "They don't stab them or gas them or anything. They just leave them in cold rooms, or slip a little something into their bottles. Some babies get a lethal shot in the night."

"Are you sure?" Kayla questioned.

"Why do you think I couldn't stand to go back there?" she yelled. "The unhealthy don't get a chance, but the very healthy babies are being genetically enhanced."

"What do you mean?"

"They're transgenic, given genes for night vision from cats. Dog genes are spliced in to give them heightened smell and hearing. I wonder if they'll ever be able to give them wings. I'm sure they must be working on it." She giggled, then frowned. "They do it quietly. Behind closed doors. Most of the time their parents don't even know."

Could this be true, or was her mother hallucinating?

"How do you know all this?" Kayla asked.

"I know it because I've seen it," her mother answered. "Things I saw at the hospital made me suspicious. Today a friend of mine, a nurse, showed me things that proved it."

"Did you tell Dad what you suspected?"

Her mother covered her face with her hands as she nodded. "I told him . . . I told him the night before . . . the night before he killed himself."

Kayla's skin popped with cold gooseflesh. "Is that why you say the bar code killed him?"

Mrs. Reed shook her head, her face awash with tears. "Not at first. At first it was because I thought the things I told him were more than he could bear. But now that I've seen his file, I know it was more. It was the part about the schizophrenia. Grandma Cathy was a schizophrenic." Her mother's head fell forward into her hands. "She died in an institution in Los Angeles."

"But Dad wasn't that way," Kayla said. "It would have shown up by now if he was."

"Maybe," her mother said, looking up at Kayla. "But it doesn't mean *you* might not become schizophrenic, start hearing and seeing things that aren't there."

Suddenly nauseated, Kayla gripped the couch. Seeing things that weren't there. Her visions. That's exactly what she'd been doing!

"You were covered under the bureau's insurance. They don't want to pay for your future drugs, maybe for your institutionalization, for your psychiatric bills. So they made his life so miserable that they hoped he'd quit." She laughed with a touch of hysteria. "Well, he quit all right. He quit the whole damned world."

Kayla's stomach flipped and she raced up to the bathroom, vomiting in the hall before she got there. As she leaned against the wall, her mind raced. What kind of world was this becoming? There must be something like this in the Thorns' codes, too. They were being shut out of everything because their bar codes revealed illness of one kind or another.

And now she *was* going crazy, just like her father's bar code had predicted. How could she fight back? How could she resist if she was insane? And that gene for schizophrenia would be encoded right on her wrist for everyone to see.

If she didn't get the code, she couldn't make a move. And if she *did* get it — the world wouldn't want her. It didn't want to pay her insurance.

This sickening realization — this unbearable feeling of being counted out — is what her mother had been trying to protect her from. The knowledge that her daughter had no future is what had been slowly destroying her. A surge of sympathy rose inside her, compassion for her tormented mother.

The smoke alarm screamed its deafening whoop. She smelled something burning an instant afterward. Something was burning — and whatever it was smelled hideous. "Mom!" she shouted, racing downstairs.

She was answered with a horrific scream from the kitchen. Her mother stood by the stove, her sleeve flaming. "I'll burn it off!" she shrieked. "Burn it!"

Kayla grabbed a pot from the stove and turned on the kitchen tap. "Drop down and roll," she screamed to her mother as the pot filled way too slowly.

Her mother stumbled backward into the side window, in too much pain to speak. The curtain lit and the flame quickly climbed to the valance.

Kayla flung the water from the pot at her mother. It dampened the flames at the bottom of her sleeve but the fire at her shoulder seemed to burn even more furiously. Her mother staggered toward the living room, fanning her clothing.

Running behind her, Kayla knew she needed something to slap out the fire. She yanked down the heavy living room drapes, tossing them on her mother.

Her mother fell to the floor and Kayla rolled her in the drapes — as a wall of flames roared in from the kitchen.

CHAPTER 15

Slowly, Kayla grew aware of a painful pounding at the front of her forehead. Nearby, she heard voices speaking in low tones. The pounding inside her head grew so intense that she couldn't bear to open her eyes. She focused on the voices as a way to distract herself from the pain.

"Nurse, when her records arrive, let me know," a male voice spoke. "I'll do the tattoo then."

"What if she regains consciousness before then?" a woman — the nurse — asked.

"Sedate her. She's over seventeen and she has no tattoo. This is for her own good. It's either tattoo her or turn her over to the Globalofficers."

"Is that the law now, doctor?"

"Yes. And now she has no parents to insist she get tattooed."

Kayla squeezed her eyes together. No parents? *No parents?*

The events of the night before suddenly came back to her. The fire. The wall of flames screaming in from the kitchen. Her mother? Where was her mother?

She forced her eyes open. The bright overhead hospital light made the pounding even worse. She became aware of a smoky, acrid smell and realized it was her own hair.

Was her mother somewhere in the hospital, in the burn unit? Pushing up on her elbows brought on a fit of hard coughing.

The doctor and nurse hurried to her side. "She's inhaled a lot of smoke," the doctor said to the nurse.

When the coughing subsided, Kayla turned toward them. "My mother?" she asked.

"Sorry, dear," the doctor said. "She didn't make it."

"No!" Kayla wailed. "No." It couldn't be true. She sank back onto the bed and turned her face into the pillow, soaking it with tears.

A firm hand clasped her arm tightly. Before she could lift her head, a needle stung her upper arm. She tried to turn but didn't have the strength as she spiraled into darkness.

When Kayla opened her eyes again, the room was a dusky gray. She felt more relaxed than ever in her life, as if no muscle were even slightly tense. Then someone coughed and she slowly turned toward the sound.

A middle-aged woman lay in a bed several feet away from her. She slept uneasily, moving frequently. Kayla remembered that she was in the hospital, and then she remembered everything.

Her mother was dead and they were going to code her.

She checked her wrist. No bar code — they hadn't done it yet. Her vision was hazy and everything in the room was blurred.

Two bright and white forms entered the room. "She's awake," the nurse spoke softly to a second nurse. "She's still feeling the effects of the sedative, I'm sure."

"Just keep her calm while I get Dr. Andrews," the second nurse replied, leaving the room. "He's licensed to code."

Kayla worked to pull herself to full consciousness. Somehow she had to throw off this drugged state and think clearly. *Straighten up*, she silently commanded herself.

Dr. Andrews would come in and tattoo her and then there would be no more wondering what to do. It would be done. There was no way she could stop it now, not in her present condition — maybe not even in any condition.

A jolt of panic ran through her. This was it — the beginning of the end of her life. The mark of mental illness would be on her. The mark of this or any serious illness would forever exclude her from real achievement in life because no one would ever want to hire her for fear of having to pay her doctor bills.

There was no avoiding the tattoo now.

Why bother caring? she thought. Her parents were both dead. She'd never see Amber again.

Zekeal had betrayed her. What was left for her to fight for?

This was too big to fight, too powerful. It was bound to win in the end. It was a kind of relief to stop fighting against it.

Something in the room crashed.

"Oh, my God!" the nurse cried.

PART 2

**When the way comes
to an end, then change —
having changed, you
pass through.**

I Ching

CHAPTER 16

The patient beside Kayla had begun to convulse so violently that she crashed onto the floor.

"Hurry! We need to get her downstairs right away!" a nurse said. The two nurses labored to lift the woman onto a gurney. They hurried her out of the room.

Kayla waited until they were gone, then hauled her legs over the side of the bed. Her knees buckled as she tried to stand and she had to grasp the bed rails to keep from landing on the floor. *Stay up, don't fall*, she urged herself.

With this unexpected opportunity, all her resolve returned. It didn't matter if she couldn't fight this, if it was hopeless. Right now she had to get out of the hospital, get somewhere away from this doctor with his code license. She moved now on simple survival instinct.

Steadying herself on one object and then the next — from bed rail to table to trash bin to chair — she made her way out of the room and headed down the hall. *Walk. Walk. Walk,* she chanted silently. *Don't think, just keep moving.*

Passing a bank of mirrors by an elevator, she

saw herself. Lines of dried scrapes were raked across her cheeks and chin. Her long brown hair was singed and matted with soot. It hung in blackened clumps around her face.

A man in green scrubs turned to look at her as she hurried past the mirrors and down the hall. She avoided eye contact and moved along.

She slowed at the open door to a patient's room. A dirty black suit and white shirt hung just inside the room, which appeared to be empty. She stepped inside and shut the door as a wave of drugged fatigue knocked her onto the bed.

If she lay down, she knew she'd sleep. That couldn't happen, she couldn't let it. Quickly, she peeled off her hospital gown and dressed in the old suit. It nearly fit, though she had to roll up the pant legs and tighten the belt past its last hole.

She slipped into the man's shoes, which were several sizes too big, and tucked her hair into the jacket collar.

Appearing casual was the key to getting out undetected, she decided as she left the room. With the sedatives still coursing through her bloodstream she couldn't go fast, anyway. That was probably a good thing because otherwise she might bolt for the door and attract attention.

The glass door whooshed open, letting her pass. It was a cool evening, almost dark.

Nausea swirled in the pit of her stomach. Foul

fluid filled her mouth, rising up from her insides. Determination carried her across the parking lot, out to the busy road.

A car horn blared as she staggered across the road. With her head down against the blinding halogen headlights, she headed for a stand of pines on the other side. Once she was deeply enclosed within the trees, her stomach lunged and she threw up. Dropping to her knees, she passed out.

In the dream, Kayla was eight again. Her mother had just dished them out each a bowl of ice cream and they sat at the table, side by side. Kayla's crayons were spread on the table as she worked on the picture in front of her. She finished the brown hair surrounding the face she was drawing and held it up. "It's you, Mommy."

"Me?" Her mother was delighted. "It's really good, Kayla. You're so talented."

"I'm going to be an artist when I grow up," Kayla said as she climbed on her mother's lap.

Her mother smoothed her hair and kissed her forehead. "You can be whatever you want to be, Kayla. You'll be a wonderful artist if that's what you'd like to do."

She wrapped her small arms around her mother's neck. "I love you, Mommy."

"I love you, too. I'll always love my Kayla."

*   *   *

The cold awakened her, but her mother's voice was still in her head. There were headlights and car noises nearby. She lay among the pines blanketed in deep blackness.

I'll always love my Kayla. She was grateful for this dream memory. It was a gift to live this moment again, a moment when her mother had still been herself.

Kayla's face contorted into a twisted mask of sorrow. Even though her mother hadn't been well, somehow Kayla had always believed there would be better times ahead and that her mother would be able to struggle out of her pain and back to her former self. That possibility was over now. She'd never see her mother again. The pain, the loss of that chance, was more than she could stand.

A wrenching, pain-filled sob shook her. Another, then another wracked her body. These gave way to a rush of tears that seemed to come from some limitless source of misery deep inside her. She cried, facedown in the cold and darkness, until she again fell to sleep.

When she awoke, she realized that the drugged feeling had mostly passed. Her hand could now curl into a fist and it wasn't as hard to move her legs. Her stomach rumbled. The last time she'd eaten was at Zekeal's place.

There was something in the pocket of her suit jacket and she fished it out, an e-card belonging to

John James. Would he mind if she bought herself something to eat? Probably. But she had to eat.

It was a two-mile walk to the all-night diner down by the river. When she got there, she suddenly felt self-conscious about her appearance, but hunger drove her inside. "Do you take e-cards?" she asked the woman at the front register. "My dad gave me his to use."

The blond woman in her twenties eyed her suspiciously. "No tattoo?"

"I turn seventeen next month," Kayla replied. She showed the card, and the woman nodded. "Sit down over there."

She ordered a hamburger, fries, and a Coke. Food had never tasted so delicious before. In the booth behind her, a woman spoke on her small phone.

"Hi, it's Katie. Listen, I'm on my way. I just stopped for some supper. I'm taking the Superlink as far as Roscoe, then I'll jump on the Thruway," she said. "I'll be there before midnight. Okay. See you then."

Katie stood and took her e-card from her wallet. There was no tattoo on her wrist.

Kayla summoned her nerve. This woman had an honest, kind face. "Excuse me," Kayla said to her. "I need a ride. Could I possibly get one from you?"

"Where you going?" Katie had long brown hair tied back in a ponytail. She was attractive, but her skin was weathered and creased with fine lines. She was probably in her early thirties.

"Um . . . just past Roscoe, to my aunt's house."

Katie stared at Kayla, taking in Kayla's dirty man's suit, her bruised face. "How old are you?"

"Seventeen next month." It seemed like a good way to avoid the bar code issue.

"You running away from home?"

"No."

"You sure about that?"

"My parents are dead." Saying the words caused her voice to catch. She couldn't think about her parents' deaths anymore, though. If she dissolved into mourning now, she wouldn't be able to think, to survive. All that had to be pushed down under the level of consciousness.

If Katie had noticed the shake in her voice, she gave no indication. "Okay. Pay your bill and come on," she said. "I have to get going."

Kayla sat in Katie's tractor-trailer, squinting at the oncoming headlights. "Ever take the Superlink before?" Katie asked.

"Once, a few years ago. My parents and I went camping on Lake George."

"It's pretty up there. The Thruway used to be the fastest way to go north, but now the Superlink is so much faster. You can drive so fast that it cuts your time in half." The speedometer revealed that they were traveling at 140 miles per hour.

"Where does it end?" Kayla asked.

"The Canadian border. Why do you want to know?"

"Just curious."

"Are you in some kind of trouble?" Katie asked her. "Running away from something?"

Was she in trouble? Not really. She didn't think so. All she'd done was sneak out of a hospital. Was that a crime? "I'm on my own. That's all," she answered.

"I see," Katie said. "Planning on getting coded next month?"

Kayla glanced into the rearview mirror and watched Katie's eyes, reflected there. Was this a trap of some kind? Could she be honest with this woman? She hadn't made up her mind yet. "I noticed *you* don't have a tattoo," Kayla mentioned.

"Nope. But that doesn't answer my question."

"I just want to know. Why don't you?"

"Cancer. It runs in my family. So I decided it would be best not to walk around with that fact tattooed on my arm."

Kayla looked at her sharply. She knew about her genes being in there. How?

Katie smiled, seeming to read her unspoken question. "I used to work for GlobalInsurance. You hear things. Your complete genetic history is in that bar code. Did you know that?"

"Yeah. I just found out. It explains a lot of what I see going on around me," she replied.

"Most people aren't aware of that," Katie said. "The insurance company wants to keep it a big secret. How did you find out?"

"My dad worked for the FBI. My mother was a nurse. They figured it out."

"When did they die?"

"Dad killed himself in March. My mom just died last night." As she spoke, a tear slid down her cheek.

"God, I'm sorry," Katie sympathized. "You've sure been through it, haven't you?"

Kayla nodded. "I guess so."

Back in March she'd thought her world was collapsing because she had no scholarship to art school. How ridiculous it seemed now, two months later. Since then she'd sustained so many losses. Before her father's death, she would never have believed that life as she'd known it could change so fast.

"Funny what happens to you once you break free of the regular world," Katie said.

"What do you mean?"

"I have a feeling you're going to find out."

After another hour of driving, Katie treated Kayla to pie and milk at the Roscoe Diner. "Have you told anyone about the genetic code being in the bar code?" Kayla asked as she broke into her pie.

"Tried to," Katie answered. "I sent a letter to a newspaper. It never got printed."

"I wonder why," Kayla said.

"Global-1 has a lot of influence with the papers. Information like that would scare people. They might not get tattooed," Katie said, wiping a milk mustache from her lips. "They probably want everyone tattooed before they give them the news. Our world is changing, big-time."

"It isn't right. It's so harsh," Kayla said. "No one can control their genes."

"Not yet they can't," Katie said. "But scientists are working on designer genes and they're getting closer by the day. Soon, if you're rich enough, you'll be able to have your unborn baby's genes altered. Not only can you make their genes perfect, you'll be able to make them better than humanly perfect. They'll be able to see in the dark and run like the wind. The gene rich will get even richer."

"But what about now?" Kayla questioned. "If you fall to the bottom of society now, you'll never be able to climb back up."

Katie nodded. "It's a brave new world, kiddo. And a scary one." She slipped her e-card from her wallet. "Might as well use this while I can. These won't be around much longer, and once they're gone we'll all be screwed." She then took a paper from her wallet. Placing it on the table, she kept her hand over it.

Kayla looked at her with questioning eyes. Katie checked quickly over her shoulder before speaking. "I'm going to give you something that will be useful," she said. She raised her hand just enough for Kayla to see the fake, rub-on tattoo beneath. It was a rub-on bar code tattoo.

"Go to the bathroom and put this on," she instructed in a low voice. "I know you're seventeen, so don't argue. And don't mess it up. It's my last one and they're hard to come by."

Kayla put her hand on the table and Katie slid the fake tattoo to her. She hurried to the bathroom and carefully pressed it on with a wet paper towel. The sight of it on her arm was chilling to her. It looked absolutely real.

When she returned, Katie had ordered some sandwiches and bottled water. She handed them to Kayla and nodded approval at the sight of the fake on Kayla's outstretched arm. "Listen, I'll take you to Binghamton with me, if you want," she said. "But my advice to you is to go straight up the Superlink and get as far away from here as fast you can. Be careful who you get in with, though. Even though you're seventeen — and, as I said, I know you are — it's still a dangerous world out there."

"How did you know my age?" Kayla asked.

Katie pulled a newspaper from her jacket pocket — the late edition of *The North Country News*. She opened it, revealing the front-page picture.

"Oh, God!" Kayla gasped.

GLOBALOFFICERS SEEK TEEN FOR QUESTIONING

Yorktown, NY. May 22, 2025 — Global-officers are seeking 17-year-old Kayla Marie Reed for questioning in the death of her mother, 43-year-old Ashley Reed, a York-town resident. The Globalofficers wish to interrogate Ms. Reed regarding the cause of the fire that destroyed the home she shared with her mother at 48 Spears Way. Two other homes on either side of the attached row house were damaged in the blaze.

Globalofficers and Emergency Medical Workers responded to the fire at 4:00 A.M. this morning, after a neighbor called in the alarm. By then the mother and daughter were unconscious, lying on a rain-soaked carpet by the front door. Mrs. Reed was badly burned and was pronounced dead immediately. "What saved the girl was the fact that she had been out in the rain and was soaked. The wet carpet she fell upon was a plus as well," said Fire Chief Don Mathers.

Dr. Maynard Andrews of Tri-County Hospital revealed that Ashley Reed suffered from smoke inhalation and lacerations. "I was about to administer the bar code to Kayla Reed when she disappeared from the hospital. She was heavily sedated and I can't imagine how she walked out. In her condition, she can't have gotten very far."

Teachers at Winfrey High describe Ms. Reed as an average student with an aptitude for art. Principal Alex Kerr said Ms. Reed's schoolwork had fallen in the last few months since becoming involved with a group connected to Decode, the bar code protest group spearheaded by Senator David Young of Massachusetts.

"We are not charging Ms. Reed with a crime at this time," said Officer Thomas Meehan of the Yorktown Globalofficers. "But neighbors say they heard the girl and her mother quarreling in the early morning, shortly before the fire. We would like to find out exactly what happened. Since Ms. Reed is untattooed — which is now a criminal offense — we have every legal right to bring her in."

The Globalofficers request that anyone seeing Kayla Reed (pictured above) please call the Yorktown Globalofficers immediately.

CHAPTER 17

The Superlink would take her to the Adirondack Park, where she knew resistance groups were hiding. If she found no one there to help her, she might continue on to Canada. Hopefully, she'd be able to cross the border without trouble.

The Superlink blazed like daylight but she'd never hitched a ride before, and the tractor-trailers sped by so fast she couldn't imagine them ever being able to stop for her. They kicked up a hot wind that blew pebbles and debris into her face and knocked her back.

By sunrise, the stolen shoes had blistered her feet beyond walking, so she tossed them into the woods behind her. Making herself a nest of old leaves among the trees, she lay down to a dreamless sleep. Hunger and daylight awoke her several hours later. Standing, she saw a Globalofficers car pass and she stepped behind a tree.

Maybe she should just go back. What was the sense of running? She hadn't killed her mother. Her only crime was not having the bar code.

They'd tattoo her, of course. It would cast its shadow on everything she tried to do with her life.

Still, she might be okay for a while. Like Amber, she'd still be able to buy things like food and gas. With the tattoo, she might even patch things up with Zekeal. If that happened, she could possibly even move in with him.

It shocked her that she would even think like that. After what she knew about him, how could she? But she pictured his handsome face, his large brown eyes and — despite what had happened — she longed to feel his arms around her. It was hard to fall out of love with him when everything had happened so suddenly.

But why couldn't he have told her the truth — that he was a member of Tattoo Gen? Had he ever loved her at all, or was it all some manipulative seduction, a trap?

In the distance, truck brakes squealed and Kayla looked toward the sound. Peering through the trees, she saw the orange roof of a Super Eatery, the road stops that appeared about every twenty or so miles along the Superlink.

Stones cut her bare feet as she made her way through the woods to the Super Eatery. They wouldn't let her in barefoot, so she went and found the painful shoes. Putting them on brought tears to her eyes.

Although each step was torture, in ten long minutes she was nearly to the Eatery. It was turning into a warm day and she slipped the jacket off. She stepped into the restaurant and the warm smell of bacon cooking and the friendly chatter of people made her long for normal life.

At the slick, bright orange counter, she ordered a cup of tea. The waitress looked at her skeptically, which reminded Kayla how bad she looked with her knotted, tangled hair, scraped face, and dirty, rumpled man's outfit.

On the wall above the counter, a large flat-screen played the news station. A blond woman in a bright pink suit stood in the corner of the screen, recounting recent newsworthy events.

President Loudon Waters's face appeared behind the woman. He was receiving honors from a scientific society for lifting all bans on human cloning, saying it was long overdue and that fear of cloning was a remnant of the past. Kayla wasn't sure how she felt about this, but at that moment she had other things on her mind.

The tea arrived and felt like hot silk going down. Her plan was to finish it and then make her phone call to the Globalofficers to turn herself in.

Another story came on about the latest space shuttle. It was now making regular stops to the new station on the moon. This shuttle was carrying a team of scientists experimenting with the impact of weightlessness on cell division.

Kayla stopped listening. She needed to plan what to say to the Globalofficers. Where would she claim to be living now? Technically, she was still a minor until she turned eighteen. There was no relative she could go to. Would the Globalofficers want to put her in some kind of institution? Juvenile hall?

The thought made her shudder. How would she survive in a place like that? She couldn't go, there wasn't a chance. *Stop, if that's what you have to do, you have to do it,* she forced herself to think. She *had* to call them. It was the only sensible thing.

The woman on the flat-screen kept talking and Kayla half listened as she finished her tea. Due to another terrorist threat, the mayor of Washington, D.C., was proposing that a protective wall be built around the city to help defend it in case of an emergency. "I've conferenced with President Waters on this and he fully endorses the measure," the mayor explained to a reporter.

The news cut away to a commercial for a new holographic screen that would present programs as though you were watching a play in your own home. The characters would be about half the size of real people. Kayla had to admit it was pretty impressive.

The programs will probably all be sponsored by Global-1, though, she reasoned. She imagined her own version of their ad. *Global-1, bringing you all the bar code has to offer — total invasion of privacy reaching down into the very intimate spiral of your DNA.*

Looking away, she scanned the group for someone who looked approachable enough to ask to borrow their phone. Her mother once told her that, when she was young, you could find a public phone, insert a metal coin, and make a call. It had never existed in Kayla's lifetime, but she wished it did. A public phone would have solved her problem now.

An elderly couple in a booth caught her attention. The woman was heavy with a halo of white fluff for hair. The man, though very old, was still strong-looking, with a shiny bald head. They spoke to each other pleasantly as they ate their pancakes. Kayla considered approaching them, but as she got up from her seat, a familiar voice made Kayla freeze, then slowly turn toward the flatscreen.

Nedra was on the screen.

"Yes, she told me she planned to set the fire," the girl told a reporter. "I didn't believe she'd really do it, though. If I had, I'd have called the Globalofficers immediately. But she's sort of a crazy type, always thinking and saying weird things, you know. She often talked about how much she hated her mother. But I never thought she'd try to kill her!"

Kayla covered her mouth with her hand as shock and disbelief swept though her.

Her picture filled the screen. It was her school picture, the way she'd looked last September. Her brown hair glistened with its neat blue streaks brushed to a sheen. Her expression was open and carefree. Kayla barely recognized herself.

Hopefully, no one else would, either.

"Globalofficers have been searching for Kayla Marie Reed since May twenty-second" the blond announcer said. "She is wanted for arson and in connection to Ashley Reed's death in that fire."

Kayla got off her stool and backed up. She had to get out of there! She whirled around and crashed into a waitress with a tray of hot coffee. The coffee splashed on her, burning her arm and hand. "Sorry!" the waitresses cried.

A waitress hurried out from behind the counter with ice wrapped in a towel. She guided Kayla to a stool and pressed the iced towel on her arm. The cold towel covered the fake tattoo and Kayla was grateful that she had it. "Thank you," she told the waitress.

Another waitress arrived with a first aid kit. "I have something that's great for burns," she said. "It's the latest thing, just came out." In a flash, she smeared the cool cream onto Kayla's arm.

Kayla watched in horror as the cream smeared and blurred the black lines of the fake bar code. She clamped her opposite hand over the ruined fake. "I have to go," she said, getting off the stool.

"You should sit a while," one of the waitresses urged her, not seeming to have noticed the damage to the tattoo.

"No, thanks. I can't," Kayla insisted, hurrying away from the waitresses.

Kayla kept her head down, barely daring to breathe. She rushed to the front lobby, then checked to see if anyone was looking at her.

Life seemed to be going on as usual. She noticed no one approaching, no one staring.

She was interested to see a robotic cashier in the lobby. She'd read that the Super Eateries would be using them. Robots had been used to do construction and factory work for years now, but they had recently become sophisticated enough for more high-level jobs. This seemed like a lucky break. A robot wouldn't remember seeing her.

Kayla paid with the e-card and walked out into the parking lot, blinking against the morning sun. Her stolen shoes bit into her heels and her burned arm throbbed.

A Globalofficers car came off the Superlink and slowly cruised the lot. Kayla turned her back toward it. Her every instinct was to run, but she knew that would only catch their attention.

A green hybrid electric-gas car stood beside her. Kayla noticed a scrap of red plaid sticking out of its door. The car couldn't be locked with that material wedged in it. Moving closer, she opened the door and slipped into the backseat. The red plaid belonged to a blanket. Kayla squeezed down into the space behind the front seat, curling up into the tightest ball she could manage. Then, reaching up, she pulled the blanket over her.

She could hide this way and maybe even — if no one noticed her — catch a ride farther north.

"Stop!" Outside the car a voice yelled angrily. "Stop this minute!"

Someone opened the car door and jumped in, quickly starting the engine. "Come on," he shouted and another person rushed into the passenger side of the car.

Kayla didn't dare look to see who was driving as the car shot out of the parking lot at top speed. At almost the same time the car started, a Global-officers siren shrieked.

CHAPTER 18

"Toz, dear, we have a stowaway." Kayla looked up into the grandmotherly face she'd seen in the restaurant.

"What?" Toz snapped without slowing.

The woman shot Kayla a quick smile, then shifted her attention to the back windshield. "They're not even chasing us, dear."

The car slowed to a less breathtaking speed. "Thank goodness," the woman said. "We'd never have outrun them in this old hybrid." Kayla lifted herself up onto the backseat.

"Now who the hell is this, Mava?" Toz demanded.

"Who are you, dear?" Mava asked Kayla.

Kayla felt delighted and a little amused that the woman didn't seem particularly alarmed or angry to find her in their car. "My name is . . ." she began and then remembered that they'd been in the Eatery and might have seen the news report. ". . . Amber Thorn."

"Nice to meet you."

"Are the Globalofficers after you?" Kayla asked. "I heard the sirens and all."

"Yes, Amber dear. Yes, I'm afraid they are," Mava replied. "Are they after you, too?"

Suddenly, Kayla felt like laughing. This was so bizarre. "Yes," she said. "They're after me."

"And why is that?" Mava asked.

"They think I set my house on fire," she answered, unable to lie to this open, direct woman. "They think I did it to kill my mother. But I didn't. I swear I didn't. She set the house on fire when she tried to burn her tattoo off her wrist."

"Oh, my goodness," Mava sympathized, her bright blue eyes growing dark. "That's terrible. You poor thing." She reached out and her eyes fixed on Kayla's red, burned hand and wrist with its smear of black lines. She said nothing but just squeezed Kayla's hand.

The kind, motherly gesture brought tears of gratitude to Kayla's eyes, but she was distracted by Mava's wrist, which bore a red, twisted scar. Mava smiled sadly. "Toz and I also removed our tattoos. I understand what your mother must have been feeling," she explained with the same lovely calmness that characterized her whole speech pattern. "However, we used acid. That was awful enough, let me tell you. Oh, so painful. But we know too many people who've done terrible damage with fire."

"Yeah, they had TMB," Toz said, shouting like a person who is hard of hearing.

"Do you mean TMP, Tattoo Mania Psychosis?" Kayla recalled.

"No! I mean TMB — Too Much Bull. That's what this Global-1 business is and it doesn't take smart people a long time to figure it out."

"Acid seems to be the best way to go," Mava went on.

"How's your hip doing?" Toz asked Mava.

She patted his shoulder lovingly. "Barely a twinge today." She turned to Kayla. "I fell and broke my hip a while back. We didn't dare go to the hospital, because once you're over eighty — I was eighty-one last January — you don't come out of the hospital."

"What do you mean?" Kayla asked. "I know of people in their eighties who have operations and then come out. My friend Amber's grandmother was eighty-five last year and had her appendix removed and was fine afterward."

"Aren't *you* Amber?" Mava asked.

"Oh, sorry. I lied. I'm Kayla."

"Oh, I see. Well, things have changed since last year. No one talks about it, but old people know that doctors now slip you something and say you died in your sleep. The insurance companies encourage them to do it because nursing homes have become too expensive. Our daughter is a doctor — she told us all about it."

"That's horrible," Kayla said.

"We certainly thought so. Our Sarah won't do it and it's made things very difficult for her. She's relocated to Toronto where the bar code isn't the law. Sarah set my hip before she left and it's doing quite well."

"Why were the Globalofficers after you?" Kayla asked.

"We didn't pay for our breakfast. Can't. No money left in our e-cards. We're heading up to Toronto to be near Sarah. They still use cash there, you know. Where are you headed?"

"I want to join a resistance group in the Adirondack Mountains."

"That's right on our way. We can drop you. But do you mind if we stop at Sarah's apartment first? She left in a hurry and we said we'd pick things up for her. Do you mind?"

"No, not at all. Thank you." Kayla curled up in the small backseat and let the car rock her. She imagined being a baby in a cradle, rocked by a loving hand. Back and forth. Back and forth. Back and . . .

* * *

They are inside the city now. Glass-and-steel buildings tower, making her feel like a mouse running along a baseboard. It's intimidating. It's probably meant to be. The wide boulevards swarm with people. She reaches out and takes the hand of the young man beside her. "Scared?" he asks, only she hears his voice in her mind. She nods. He rubs her shoulders. "Don't be. This will work."

* * *

A bump in the road rocked her from her vision.

Sitting up, she saw they were approaching a toll. "Belt up and get as low as you can," Toz told them.

"Why?" Kayla asked. "What's —"

Toz speeded up, driving the car to its 140-mile-per-hour limit. Kayla was knocked down again into her seat. It was probably best to stay down as Toz directed, so she covered her head and drew herself tightly into a ball.

"Woo-hoo!" Toz shouted triumphantly as he blasted through the bar blocking his way at the tollbooth. Kayla saw shards of wood fly up in all directions. An alarm whooped, but Toz never let up on the gas pedal. A Globalofficers siren started up.

"Stay down!" Toz shouted to them. "I've got a good lead and the turnoff's in two miles."

Toz drove at full speed all the way to the exit he wanted. He raced straight through a clump of trees, slammed on the brakes, and shut the engine. The Globalofficers raced on, going straight up the Superlink.

Toz chuckled gleefully.

"Fine driving, dear," Mava praised him. "How are you feeling?"

"Perfectly fine," he said gruffly. "Stop worrying. I've never been better."

"Toz had a heart attack last year," Mava told Kayla. "Thank God it was last year and not this year."

"My heart is in perfect condition now," Toz growled as he started the car and they pulled out of the trees, back onto the exit ramp. "These little hybrids were good cars in their day. I don't know why they stopped making them."

Mava sighed. "The big oil companies didn't want people to stop using gas, I suppose."

They drove to Albany, straight to the modern apartment building where Sarah had lived. When Mava shut the lobby door behind them, Kayla felt safe for the first time in days.

Inside, Toz unlocked the door of an apartment. "She certainly did leave quickly," Mava commented as she stepped into the living room. A lamp still lit the beige, modern furniture. A cup of coffee stood half full on the sleek glass coffee table.

"Make yourself at home," Mava told her. "The shower is just down the hall."

In the bathroom, it felt good to peel off her filthy clothing. Kayla stepped into the warm flowing stream of the shower and never before had she felt so blessed to be washed clean, to have her shoulders thumped by water. She pressed her body into the tile wall and let the water run down her aching body.

Sarah had left all her toiletries behind. When Kayla was done, she stepped out and let the clean, thick towels mop the wetness from her body. She slipped into the white terrycloth robe that hung on the back of the door and used Sarah's deodorant and moisture creams. She used a bath oil to wipe away the last of the fake tattoo. Only a few days ago she'd taken these things for granted. Now they seemed like lovely and rare luxuries.

As she stepped out of the bathroom, Mava came toward her with scissors. "How would you feel about a haircut?" she asked. "It would make you less identifiable. I'm pretty good at it."

Kayla fingered her wet hair. "Okay," she agreed.

She sat at a vanity in Sarah's elegant bedroom. Mava cut, catching the hair on a towel at her feet. Kayla, worried that an eighty-one-year-old woman might have a shaky grip on the scissors, wore a scowl of concern throughout the cut.

When the blow-dry was done, Kayla examined the short, wispy result. Her hazel eyes appeared to be nearly twice their size.

"Do you like it?" Mava asked. "I think it looks wonderful on you. It will be easy to take care of."

"I look like a different person," Kayla said slowly.

Mava squeezed her shoulder. "Maybe that's as it should be." She opened a closet packed with clothing, and tossed outfits onto the bed. "I'm sure Sarah has already taken the things she really wants. She recently gained some weight. These things might not even fit her anymore. You can have whatever clothing you like."

Sarah's clothing included the latest neon colors, but somehow Kayla wasn't in the mood for them anymore. Instead, she put on a pair of black stretch pants that fit her perfectly. A long-sleeved silver shirt trimmed in bright pink was her next choice. Sarah's black hiking boots were exactly her size.

"Who would have guessed that you're such a beautiful girl?" Mava commented when Kayla was dressed.

Kayla smiled at her. "Thank you. Does Sarah have a computer I could use?"

May 23, 2025
From: DrS@globalnet.planet
To: (AT)cybercafe1700@globalnet.planet

This message is for Amber Thorn — I don't know if she's there right now. If someone gets it, could you keep it for her? Maybe you could leave it behind the counter or something.

Amber, you might have heard some news about me. It is not true and I am fine. I miss you. I hope you are well and that Aunt Miserable isn't driving you too nuts.

Love, K.

From: DrS@globalnet.planet
To: MFTaylor@globalnet.planet

Everything you read about me is a lie. I am okay but I won't be back. I hope that somehow, someday we meet again. I am grateful for your friendship. Don't trust Zekeal. He and Nedra are spies for Tattoo Generation. Please pass this info on to Allyson and August.

Your friend, K.

From: MFTaylorsr@globalnet.planet
To: DrS@globalnet.planet

Thank God our son isn't with you. At least he's not in as much trouble as that. He disappeared the same night you set your house on fire. We are sick with worry. If you have any idea where he is, please contact us.

CHAPTER 19

Kayla shut the computer down quickly. It hadn't occurred to her at first that she could be tracked through Sarah's e-mail address. It was possible, though, especially if Mfumbe's parents went to the Globalofficers.

Where had he gone . . . and why?

Kayla walked to the living room where Toz and Mava sat watching the news. Nedra's face filled the screen. She wore a red jumpsuit — the same kind the Tattoo Gen group on the West Coast favored. Below her image, a subtitle read *Nedra Harris representing Tattoo Generation*.

With the same strong, determined attitude she'd worn when she was against the bar code, Nedra now spoke about the need for all seventeen-year-olds to get tattooed. "This is the mandate of our new millennium, which will be governed by the best, the brightest, and the most fit. Let each young person of our generation step forward and show their pride by wearing the bar code — a tattoo that marks them as part of the Global-1 team. Sadly, there are still some young people who are mistrustful of Global-1's plan for world unity. I say to these misdirected dissidents — throw off this blind mistrust and take your place in the bold new world."

Toz clicked her off and turned to Kayla. "Now aren't you glad you didn't get that damned tattoo? Wouldn't you hate to be like her?"

"I know her," Kayla revealed. "She used to be part of our Decode group."

Toz nodded, leaning back in his easy chair. "You become the monster you fear the most, so the monster won't overtake you."

"That doesn't always happen," Mava disagreed. "Not everyone is like that. Kayla hasn't become a monster. Doesn't she look pretty?"

"Damn cute," Toz agreed gruffly. "No one will recognize her, which is the point of the redesign, I suppose."

"Yes, dear," Mava agreed. "Now rest. Remember your heart."

"My heart is big and strong and belongs to you, darling," Toz told her with a playful wink.

Each morning a paper thumped against the front door and Kayla scoured it for news about herself.

The first day her story was on page three. The robot cashier at the Superlink Eatery had been programmed to identify a photographic list of wanted criminals and had automatically contacted Globalofficers saying Kayla Reed had been there. They traced the credit card from John James back to a man who had died at the Tri-County Hospital during an operation on May 21.

At least he didn't miss his e-card or his suit, Kayla thought, glad to be rid of the nagging guilt she felt for taking the man's things.

By the sixth day, her story was just a paragraph on page twelve. Kayla put the paper down and looked in the mirror. Her scrapes had all healed. Her new haircut made her look very different. Maybe everyone would just forget about her.

By Monday of the next week, Mava and Toz had moved most of Sarah's belongings into bags and stuffed them into their car trunk. Even though they were reluctant to leave, they knew their safe haven couldn't last forever. As they ate breakfast that morning, someone knocked on the door.

Kayla hurried to Sarah's bedroom and hid in the closet. After a few minutes, Mava spoke to her through the door. "It was just the landlord. He wanted to know why Sarah hadn't paid her rent." Nearly faint with relief, Kayla came back out.

"We told him she'd be back tonight," Mava went on. "So we really should leave as soon as possible."

Kayla sat on the bed to let her heartbeat return to normal. Mava sat beside her and took her hand. "Toz and I have been talking," she began. "We think you should come to Toronto with us. Although we have no money now, Sarah will help us get set up."

"Will we be able to get across the border without bar codes?" Kayla asked.

"We're not sure. If we have trouble, though, we'll find a way to call Sarah. Her boyfriend has a bar code. He can come across and we'll drive back in his car." Mava smiled sadly. "Toz won't like leaving his hybrid behind, but in the end he might have to."

"I would *love* to come with you, thank you," Kayla said, hugging Mava warmly. This was like a miracle, a new start.

Kayla was tempted to check the e-mail one last time, hoping to hear from Amber, but decided against it. It might bring the Globalofficers right to her.

Back on the Superlink, they went for miles before coming to another tollbooth. Toz knew an exit that brought him around to the other side of the toll. "Out of gas," he reported. "We can switch to electric energy for a while but we'll have to fuel up eventually."

They'd gone a number of miles and now a tollbooth lay ahead of them again. "Get ready for another breakthrough," Toz warned them excitedly. "Battle stations."

Kayla squeezed down into the backseat and covered her head. Toz threw the car into full speed.

Abruptly, the car weaved wildly out of the lane. Car horns blared and Kayla sat up. Toz had let go of the wheel and clutched his chest.

"Toz!" Mava screamed.

Toz grabbed the wheel and hit the electric speed pedal. Then he slammed forward onto the steering wheel.

A cement wall that bordered the toll lane loomed in front of them. Mava grabbed the steering wheel and pulled it, riding the car along the wall on two wheels for seconds, and then glass shattered as the car smashed onto its side and slid.

Kayla flew forward, hitting the windshield. From somewhere a siren howled.

"Toz," Mava sobbed, leaning on her husband. "Toz, wake up."

Toz lay slumped over, not responding. Mava's head was bleeding and Kayla cringed at the unnatural angle at which the old woman's arm hung.

Strobing red lights passed over them as Globalofficers cars screeched to the scene of the accident.

"Kayla," Mava cried. "Are you all right?"

"Yes, I think so," Kayla replied.

"Then get out of here now. Run. You can get away."

"I can't leave you!"

"You can't *help* us. As soon as they take us to the hospital, we're dead. Toz is dead now." Mava's blue eyes held Kayla in their gaze. "Quickly. Go."

Two Globalofficers were rapidly approaching the car. Kayla knew she couldn't do anything for Toz and Mava now. The car door above her had sprung open when they hit the wall. Pulling herself up, she climbed out.

Jumping down into a crouch, she kept low and ran along the side of the wall.

"Stop!" someone shouted. "You. By the wall. Stop now!"

Kayla ducked into the woods at the end of the wall and began to run. A gunshot blasted just beside her ear.

Dropping to the ground, Kayla scrambled on her belly through the leaves and dirt. Another shot fired. It scalped a chunk of bark from a tree just ahead of her.

She ran for cover.

CHAPTER 20

It seemed to her that she lay still a long time. Her head throbbed and blood ran down her forehead, dripping into her eyes. She blinked hard, afraid to move and wipe it away. Finally, though, the two Globalofficers left.

Getting up, she used her hand to whisk the blood from her aching forehead. Then, running in short sprints, she moved deeper into the woods, stopping occasionally to clutch her pounding head.

Heading up along the Superlink was too dangerous now. She'd have to get as deep into the trees as she could.

The last dying rays of sunset guided Kayla among the trees as she silently thanked Sarah for the hiking boots and the fleecy hooded sweater. She pulled up the hood against a cold wind that chilled her neck. Before, her long hair had always protected it. Now she felt exposed and vulnerable as the cool air ruffled her new cut. Her neck tingled with more than cold. It had snapped back hard when she'd been thrown forward in the accident.

Her stomach growled angrily. There had been nothing to eat since breakfast and she longed for food. Sitting on a flat boulder, she considered her predicament. Here in the middle of the woods, she wasn't likely to come across any food. What did she know about berries and edible plants? Exactly nothing.

A trickling sound told her that there was water somewhere nearby. Her best bet was to search for it, so she followed the sound to a very narrow stream. Kneeling, she drank, then washed her dirty, bloodstained face. For lack of a better plan, she began to follow the stream. At least she would never be too far from water that way.

The light was almost completely gone, but she continued to follow the sound of the stream a long way into the woods. She cried out as she stumbled in the dark over something hard. Lying there, she made no move to get up. Every part of her ached. The car accident had made her sore all over. The back of her neck now tingled badly.

Somewhere, someone was cooking something that smelled delicious. Sitting up, she peered in all directions. Then she saw a light, very small, about a mile off in the distance.

With the last of her strength, she made her way toward it. The cooking smell kept growing stronger, encouraging her on.

Finally, the source of the smell appeared in the darkness. A cabin with a lit sign in front, some kind of restaurant or bar. Before long she heard the loud sound of animated voices — people conversing, laughing. A warm, inviting place.

Her spirits lifting, she hurried toward the cabin. She had no way to pay for food, but she'd think of something. She looked through a window at people inside, eating, drinking, and talking to one another. A large flat-screen hung over the bar, and many people gazed up at it, watching a basketball game.

Walking around to the front, she read the sign: THE OASIS. A small parking lot held about six cars that had driven in on a narrow road that led away deeper into the forest. There were definitely more than six cars' worth of people inside the place. How had they gotten there?

She stepped inside, attracting no attention. The people were all focused on their friends or on the screen.

"We interrupt this sporting event for a brief special announcement," a voice broke into the basketball game. The spectators groaned but kept their eyes on the screen.

A blond woman in a suit appeared in the lower corner of the screen. A picture of the tollbooth where the accident had occurred filled the large screen behind her. "There was a fatal car crash at a Superlink tollbooth just outside of Albany this morning," the reporter told the audience.

Kayla stood in the doorway, staring at the screen, mesmerized by the picture on it.

"It is believed that eighty-five-year-old Tova Alan, the driver, suffered a lethal heart attack that caused him to lose control of his vehicle and slam into a cement wall," the reporter continued. "His wife, eighty-one-year-old Mava Alan, was rushed to a nearby hospital in critical condition and is not expected to live."

Although she knew this already, had faced this reality, a lump formed in Kayla's throat at the reporter's words.

"The Alans were wanted by Globalofficers for toll jumping on their trip up the Superlink. A third passenger in the car was identified as seventeen-year-old Kayla Marie Reed. Ms. Reed is currently a fugitive wanted for the homicide of her mother, Mrs. Ashley Reed. Ms. Reed fled the scene of the accident and refused to stop when summoned by Globalofficers. The charges against her now include toll jumping, failure to cooperate with Globalofficers, and suspected homicide.

"Anyone seeing Ms. Reed, who is believed to be somewhere north of Albany, New York, please call this central Globalofficers number."

Kayla's junior yearbook photo once again flashed on the screen with the Globalofficers phone number under her face. A man at the bar turned and stared at Kayla. The woman beside him turned to see what her companion was staring at.

Kayla ran her hand through her short hair as an excuse to put her arm over her face, and walked out the door. It was dark to the left of the doorway and she stepped into the shadow, slowly moving around to the left of the building. Crouching low, she waited to see if anyone rushed out after her. When no one came, she ran out into the darkness again.

She slumped down at the foot of a large pine. They'd described her as a fugitive from the Globalofficers. How had all this happened? The forest around her swirled and then everything was blackness.

Hours later she came to with a throbbing head. Her stomach was now a deep and empty cavern. The distant voices from the cabin had quieted. Maybe it was now closed for the night. Hopefully they had a Dumpster and she'd find something inside it to eat.

It wasn't easy to find her way back in the complete darkness. As she came nearer, though, she spotted a dull light. It gave her a guide to follow and brought her to the back of the place. Standing behind a tree, she looked in the window and saw that the Oasis was, indeed, closed and she was gazing into the kitchen area. Half a roasted chicken sat, uncovered, on the counter.

A breeze banged the screen door as light poured from the doorway, telling her there was no locked inside door behind the screened one. Someone must be in there. They wouldn't just go off and leave the place open and unattended.

But maybe if the person was in the front, she might be able to slip in, grab the chicken, and escape with it. Her stomach had made her desperate enough to try.

Cautiously creeping forward, staying in the shadows, she got to the open door and entered the rustic, dully lit kitchen. It was only about five feet to the chicken, but she was afraid to take the first step toward it.

A floorboard groaned under her first, anxious step and made her freeze in place. She waited for a response.

Nothing.

She took another step, then froze again as a trapdoor in the floor just several feet in front of her lifted. Two arms pushed it up. Someone was about to come up from below and they would be face-to-face in a matter of seconds.

Kayla grabbed a carving knife from a side table, clutched it tightly, and waited.

CHAPTER 21

"Oh, my God!" Kayla gasped.

The young man holding up the trapdoor looked equally shocked. "Kayla!"

"Mfumbe," she replied. It was so good to see his face. "How did you get here? I heard you were missing. Are you all right? What happened?"

He came out of the hole in the floor. "Put down the weapon and I'll tell you."

With a self-conscious smile, she put the knife down. He pulled a rough-hewn chair forward, offering her a seat. "I like your new hairdo," he said. "But the bloody face doesn't look too stellar."

He rinsed a rough white cloth in the sink and handed it to her. The warm wetness felt so good. She was amazed to see how red the cloth was when she was done.

"Could I have that chicken?" she asked as her stomach growled loudly.

"Absolutely." He stuck it on a plate and handed it to her along with a knife and fork. "How about a soda, too?" he offered, pulling a can from the refrigerator and opening it.

He wiped up the kitchen while she devoured the food ravenously. Then he pulled up a chair for himself and sat backward on it. "You've become a real celeb since I last saw you."

She laughed bitterly. "It's been a nightmare."

"I know you didn't set your house on fire," he said seriously. "What happened?"

She told him everything, reliving the awful events as she spoke.

"That's horrible," he sympathized. "My story isn't nearly as terrible, but when I got home that night my dad was waiting for me with a friend of his who's a postal bar code tattooer. He'd come to our house with all his equipment, at Dad's request. Dad demanded that I get the tattoo right then and there."

"Why?" Kayla asked.

"His tattoo pal told him the same thing your mom did about the genetic code in there. That got him thinking about how people of African descent have been so discriminated against throughout history. So he's decided this is our chance to turn the tables. Our family is apparently pretty healthy. He says that since our genes have kept us down for so many centuries, now our genes are going to advance us and we have to be ready to take advantage of this unexpected turn of events."

"It *is* sort of ironic if you think about it."

"Yeah, I know. But it's not right. I'm not going to give up everything I believe just because it suddenly looks like the bar code might work to my advantage."

Kayla glanced at his wrist and felt relieved to see no tattoo.

"I admire that a lot," she said. "I don't believe in what the bar code stands for, but it would also work against me. To be against it when you would gain from it . . . that's amazingly final level."

"Thanks," he said. "But I couldn't do it. No matter what I'd get from it, I'd feel like a prisoner."

"What happened when you said no?"

"We had a huge fight. Dad said no son of his was going to drop to the bottom of society after everything Africans had done to lift themselves up. He said, 'Get tattooed or don't expect to live in this house' — so I left. I'd heard about this place. When I was at a virtual reality site someone told me it was around here, so I drove straight up."

"Where are we?"

"The place doesn't have a name. It's just a bunch of people who don't want to be pushed around by Global-1. They live all over these woods. Some are tattooed, some aren't. Nobody cares. They trade with one another for stuff. I got this job in the kitchen and I get paid with food and clothes so I can survive. It's astral. I like it here."

"Where do you keep your car?" she asked.

"I traded it for a cabin where I live." He scowled. "How did you know I'd left?"

"I e-mailed you to warn you about Zekeal and Nedra, but you had gone. Your parents are freaked out. They're looking for you."

Mfumbe shrugged. "I hope they don't find me. I'm real happy here. What about Zekeal and Nedra?"

She told him they'd joined Tattoo Generation. "Everything seemed to go crazy from the time I found out how Zekeal was betraying everyone, especially me."

Mfumbe seemed doubtful. "I can't believe Zeke is the enemy. He and I were tight."

"Why else would he be a member of Tattoo Gen? I know for sure he *is* a member."

"I don't know. But maybe there's a reason."

They sat together for a moment without speaking. After a few minutes, he pulled a pack of peppermint gum from his shirt pocket and offered it to her.

"Thanks," she said, taking a piece.

In the morning Kayla awoke snuggled in a warm sleeping bag. She blinked to bring the simple, neat room around her into focus. Two windows on either side of the wooden door let in soft morning light. Touching her forehead, she felt clean gauze and remembered Mfumbe dabbing her cuts with hydrogen peroxide and covering them.

She wiggled from her sleeping bag, still clothed, and looked out the window. Outside, Mfumbe had built a fire and was cooking bacon in a pan. Last night when he'd led her back to his cabin, it had been too dark for her to see much. Now she noticed a picnic table with a bench on either side.

"Morning," he greeted her when she stepped

outside. He offered her a plate of bacon and eggs. "How are you?"

"Glad I ran into you," she replied, smiling softly. "I don't know what I would have done if I hadn't."

He sat beside her on the bench and ate his eggs. "You picked a perfect place to hide. These people who live in these woods would never turn you in. It's stellar the way you work together and support one another. It proves to me that bar code resisters can band together and make a difference. It reminds me of the American Revolution when people began to unite against the British."

"But they had leaders like Washington and Benjamin Franklin," Kayla said.

"We have Dave Young," he replied.

"What's he been able to do?" she scoffed.

"He's still active. They haven't shut Decode down yet."

"Maybe," she agreed doubtfully. "I was thinking of heading up to find Eutonah."

"You know, there's something we never told you — because I guess we didn't want to freak you out," he said. "When you contacted Eutonah, your site numbers never moved."

"But I saw her! She was totally real!"

"I believe you. Eutonah is a real woman. I've heard of her. But I don't think you knew of her before coming to our group. Did you?"

"No. Do you think it means I'm crazy?"

He laughed lightly. "Why would it mean that? I

think you have a gift for psychic ability. We all use such a small part of our brains at any given time. Sometimes we use one part, sometimes another. I believe we'll all eventually use our entire brain, or at least larger portions of it at once. But that will only happen if we're allowed to evolve. Maybe psychic ability will be part of that evolution. And maybe Eutonah is more highly evolved, too — so the two of you were able to connect. That might also be the way you found your way to me, here in the woods."

Kayla had learned about evolution in school. She knew the theory that living things changed in order to adapt to their environment. People had once debated the theory, but by the year 2015 it had been accepted as fact.

"What do you mean, if we're *allowed* to evolve?" she asked him. "Don't people and animals do that naturally over time?"

"Not anymore," he replied, finishing the last of his food. "Global-1 has lifted all bans on cloning. I believe that the reason they want everyone coded is to make it easy to decide who will be cloned and who won't. Once people are reproduced just as they were, evolution stops. There's no change. No adaptation. The human race won't move forward. The brain will never be used at its full capacity."

"But what about designer genes?" Kayla asked. "Doesn't that change people? They'll be able to see better, run faster, hear better, and on and on."

"That's true," he agreed. "But it will be man-made evolution. People will change in ways scientists and the government think they should. Those ways might not be the changes we really need to make."

He picked up the plates they'd used. "Come on down to the stream with me. We can wash these dishes and keep talking."

They talked for the rest of the day as they picked blueberries in the woods. At six, Mfumbe left for work, leaving her alone. She passed the time by reading from his pile of books, using lantern light. When he returned just before dawn, she awoke long enough to see him crawl into the roll of old blankets on the floor. "Good night," she said.

"Night," he mumbled. She tossed him her pillow. He tossed it back. "It's okay. Use it."

Mfumbe gave her a pad for her sketching and one morning he returned from the Oasis with a pack of playing cards. They liked to play gin rummy, but mostly they talked.

Mfumbe made so much sense to her. He had ideas about things she'd never considered. "We've been headed toward this bar code for years," he said one night as they sat around their campfire. "First came the credit cards, then driver's licenses as ID cards, then the face scanners, eye scanners, and fingerprint scanners, and those

DNA chip implants. But I think the bar code is different."

"Why?" she asked.

"Because people wear it. It's a sign of allegiance to Global-1 as well as an identifier and a genetic table."

"I guess that's true," she agreed.

"Ever since that day we were discussing how genetic sequences are sometimes represented as bar codes, I've been thinking — if our genes determine who we are, and genes look like a bar code, then we already wear a bar code tattoo. Our genes are our own unique, personal bar code tattoo."

The next morning Kayla awoke earlier than usual. Mfumbe wasn't there. He wasn't in front making breakfast as usual, either.

Kayla stepped into her boots and went outside. The forest was unnaturally still, except for one section about five yards away. A breeze blew the trees and bushes around and the colors seemed unusually vivid. She stepped toward it and a figure took form in front of her.

It was Eutonah. The woman beckoned to her with her hand.

As Kayla went closer, the image began to blur.

She sensed movement in the forest. Footsteps. A dog barked. Turning toward the sound, her heart slammed into her chest.

The woods were full of Globalofficers.

CHAPTER 22

Kayla ran, her heart pumping. "There she is!" a voice behind her shouted as she raced down to the stream, stumbling and weaving, but determined to reach Mfumbe. She found him crouched at the river's edge washing some clothing. He jumped up when she crashed through the trees. "Globalcops," she panted. "Everywhere!"

He grabbed her hand and together they splashed into the stream. The barking dogs sounded nearer every second. She followed Mfumbe out the far side of the stream. "This way," he said.

The dogs dragged Globalofficers down to the water where Mfumbe had been washing. "They must have crossed," a man shouted.

Mfumbe led her to a tumbledown shed. There was a hatch door in the ground in front of it and she helped him pull it up by its handle. Kayla climbed down wooden stairs to the bottom. Mfumbe pulled the cover over the hole before joining her.

"It's an abandoned mine shaft," he explained. "I found it one day while I was exploring."

Using the cold dirt wall as a guide, they made their way along a dark tunnel. "You should go back," she said. "They're not looking for you."

"They might be," he replied. "My parents might have them looking for me. I'm a missing person. They might be taking in everyone who lives in these woods for being uncoded."

"But you're not wanted for a crime."

He took her hand. "Not having a code is a crime."

They followed the tunnel for what seemed like a long time. When they climbed out at the end they were still in the forest, but they couldn't hear any dogs barking. "Listen, we've ditched them for now, but they know we're around," Mfumbe said. "We'd better keep moving."

He pulled a piece of rectangular black plastic with a monitor screen from his pocket. "A guy left this GPS in the Oasis yesterday. I was planning to give it back to him tonight. I guess it's mine now. It'll tell us exactly where we are and how to get where we're going. It bounces a signal off some satellites floating in space. The question now is — where are we going?"

"The Adirondack Mountains?" Kayla suggested. "I think that's the best place."

"Probably," he agreed. He pushed some buttons on the GPS and turned. "It looks like we're going that way."

They walked through the woods for the rest of the morning and into the late afternoon. Around five o'clock they came out of the woods to the back of a large grocery warehouse. The back door of a truck was open and the two of them scrambled into the vehicle.

"Soda and potato chips," Kayla read the labels on the boxes stacked in the trucks. "It could be worse. It could have been beets or something."

The door behind them slammed shut. Kayla and Mfumbe looked at each other, unsure what to do. The truck might take them farther north. "What if it's going south?" Kayla asked.

Mfumbe took his GPS from his pants pocket. "We'll know in a minute."

The engine started and they both stared at the GPS. "North," Mfumbe said. "And right up the Superlink."

"Final level," Kayla said, smiling up at him.

The truck carried them for miles. They sat with their backs against the boxes, drank soda, and ate chips as they bumped along up the superhighway. She rested her head on his shoulder and he put his arm around her. "I'm glad I found you," she said.

"Me, too," he agreed, holding her a little tighter.

When the truck finally stopped nearly two hours later, they hid behind boxes in the back as the driver carried out the freight from the front. "Stay or go?" Mfumbe checked for Kayla's opinion.

"Stay," she whispered. "We'll keep checking that thing to make sure we don't veer off course. But this truck could take us miles up the road."

They kept low until the truck motor started again. At the next stop, the driver removed four boxes, and they realized they were losing more and more of their cover at each stop. "We'd better get out or he'll see us at the next stop," Kayla said.

While the driver was delivering his order, they hurried out of the truck. They emerged into the dark night to see a neon sign announcing that they were at the Adirondack Motel. "We're here already?" Kayla asked as they ran to the back of the building.

Mfumbe checked his GPS. "We're at the bottom of the mountain range. We have to get up around Keene or Lake Placid. That's where the resistance groups are. They like being near the Canadian border — just in case things get rough."

That night they found a discarded mattress in a Dumpster at the back of the motel and dragged it into the nearby trees. "It's cold," Kayla commented.

"It's always colder up north," Mfumbe reminded her. "We've come pretty far today." He pulled her close and his body heat helped take off the chill.

Kayla awoke in the night, shivering. Several feet away a pool of moonlight broke through the trees. A figure took form in the moonlight. Eutonah was there once again. She raised her arms and seemed to be chanting, although Kayla heard no sound.

Then a voice whispered inside Kayla's mind, "Stay on my wavelength and I will pull you in."

Kayla got up and walked toward the sparkling image. But it faded slowly. By the time she reached the moonlight, there was nothing there.

In the morning she awoke and saw Mfumbe

coming across the parking lot and toward the trees, holding a brown paper bag. "Good, you're up. I was just about to wake you." He sat on the mattress beside her. "Two teas and two muffins." He lifted the food out of the bag.

"Did you steal this?" Kayla asked.

"No. I asked for it at the deli down the road. I just thought I'd take a chance and it worked. The guy gave it to me."

"Astral," she said.

"Yeah. He told me a lot of people are down on their luck around here. They've been thrown out of jobs and can't find new ones. He says it's hard times since the bar code became law."

Not everyone was as generous as the deli man. As they continued north, they began shoplifting, taking only what they needed to survive on.

The idea of stealing bothered both of them, but they could find no other way to stay alive. Kayla was amazed by how expert she had become at sneaking food and drink out of convenience stores.

At one truck stop, Mfumbe's photo stared back at them from a bulletin board. His parents were looking for him and had put up Missing Person flyers. "You should let them know you're all right," Kayla said to him.

"I'd like to let my mother know," he admitted. "But I can't think of a way to do it."

Neither could she. Without access to a computer or a phone, they were completely isolated.

Along the way they read discarded newspapers they found in garbage cans or Dumpsters. Kayla's story had nearly disappeared. Did it mean they weren't looking for her anymore? That seemed too good to really be true, but at least her picture wasn't all over the place.

David Young's picture *was* all over the papers, though. After he'd resigned from the Senate in protest over the bar code, he'd set up Decode headquarters right in Washington. "This is still a free country and I have nothing to hide," he told the press.

Kayla studied his picture in the paper, a good-looking man in his thirties with dark eyes and tousled brown hair. "He has a kind face," she observed to Mfumbe.

"He's a great guy," Mfumbe said. "I'd like to go to Washington and work for Decode."

"Washington's that way," she said, pointing south.

"I don't mean right now. I can't go now."

"Why not?"

"Because right now I'm with you," he answered.

She looked up at him and realized that the only reason he was there was because he wouldn't leave her. He was doing this for her.

She wrapped her arms around him and pressed

her cheek against his chest. He embraced her, holding tight. Then she looked up at him and they kissed.

Three weeks later, Mfumbe and Kayla walked into the town of Keene Valley, New York. Both had lost over ten pounds. The walking had made them muscular. Their hair was knotted and wild. Their gaunt faces and wiry, strong-looking bodies made people stare at them as they went down the road. Kayla thought they must look like savages from some exotic and hard place. And that was what she felt she'd turned into.

They came to a hillside nearly covered in juniper bushes and sat down, leaning against the flat side of a boulder. The juniper smelled so wonderful, although the plants' rough foliage caught at her pants, snagging them.

Kayla looked off at the towering peaks of the mountain range. It was vast and magical here.

"In another couple of weeks I would have been graduating," Mfumbe said a bit sadly, looking up at the mountains.

"That's right," she said without looking at him. She was weary, and the blue-tinted mountaintops were soothing to gaze on.

"Then I would have been off to Yale. Someone at Yale saw me on that Virtual *Jeopardy* show and offered me a scholarship on the spot." He sighed.

"They don't give scholarships to guys without bar codes."

"No wonder your dad was so determined for you to get tattooed," she commented.

"I know. I can't really blame him. But I'll be eighteen next week — no longer a minor, and my parents can't force me to do anything against my will." He was silent for a while, and Kayla let her mind go blank except for taking in the scenery in front of her.

"I love you, Kayla," he said abruptly. "I've loved you since the first day we met, on the stairs. But I could never tell you. You were so crazy about Zeke and all. I thought I loved you back then, but that was nothing compared to the way I feel about you now."

Kayla listened, growing happier with every word. They were so close now. She'd known ever since they kissed at the truck stop that day that she loved him — was *in* love with him and loved him deeply as a person, both. She knew he felt the same. Why else would he have gone through all this with her? But hearing the words made it so real, so out in the open.

And then she heard snoring.

Whirling around, she saw that he was asleep against the rock. How long had he been like that?

He was asleep but his words were still in her head as clearly as if he were saying them in front of her. But was love enough? Wasn't she only getting him into more trouble?

If that was true, she should leave him right now, while he slept and couldn't stop her. Then he could go to Washington. He wouldn't be stuck with her.

Getting up, she walked down the hillside — but stopped.

Zekeal stood there, right in front of her. He stared at her but didn't seem to see her. Was he real or a vision?

Kayla ran back to Mfumbe and shook him. "What? Wha —" he stammered as he came awake.

"Zekeal is down the hill. Over there. I saw him!"

He stood up and peered into the distance. "No one's there."

"He is! I saw him!"

"You must have been dreaming." A sad, disappointed expression overtook his face. "Dreaming about Zeke."

"I wasn't! I don't care about him anymore. You're the only one I love. But he *was* there!" She looked down the hill and saw no one. If Zekeal had been there, he was no longer present.

Mfumbe wrapped his arms around her. "You love me?"

"Yes, I do. I love you completely."

"Then there is no Zeke, no bar code tattoo, no Tattoo Gen. There's only us," he said.

CHAPTER 23

That evening Kayla knew something was wrong. Her arms and legs were heavy. Her head had become difficult to hold up and her forehead burned.

She slept for most of the next day, curled beside a boulder. Mfumbe pressed cool leaves against her brow and fed her crackers they'd saved along the way.

When she awoke the next day she felt well enough to walk into the nearby town of Keene to find food. But as they walked along the main street, she staggered.

"We have to get something to bring your fever down," Mfumbe said. Kayla pressed her palm into his and leaned against the cool bricks of the building for support. "You're burning up," he said, sweeping his hand along her cheek. "We just passed a drugstore. I'll go back to it and grab some medicine."

"I should do it. I'm better at this than you are," she argued when they were in front of the drugstore. "You almost got caught last time."

"No. You're too sick. You won't be quick enough." They walked up a side alley. "Wait here," he told her.

Mfumbe went in the side door and Kayla followed, despite his advice. "The medicine is all the way in front," she whispered to him. "The cash register is up there. They'll see you."

"Not if I do it right," he insisted. "Stay here and pretend to look at greeting cards."

He strolled casually to the front. "Hi, there," the man behind the register greeted him, although there was only suspicion in his voice.

"Hi," Mfumbe replied. "Do you have thermometers?"

"Over there, by the Adlevenol."

Mfumbe went to where the thermometers were stacked. As he stared up at them, he palmed a box of Adlevenol and slipped it into his pants pocket. "Can I help you?" the man asked aggressively. He hadn't taken his eyes off Mfumbe the whole time.

"You don't have the kind I'm looking for," Mfumbe told him.

Kayla pretended to look at cards by the front door and stole furtive glances at the man behind the counter. She didn't like the expression on his face. He wasn't happy about Mfumbe being in his store. He suspected him.

"There are more thermometers in the third aisle," the man told Mfumbe.

"Okay. I'll go check those out," Mfumbe said.

The man bent down behind the counter. Kayla shifted from foot to foot. He was out of sight for too long. What was he doing under there?

Mfumbe was in the third aisle, keeping up the charade of looking for thermometers.

Something was wrong.

Kayla went to Mfumbe in the third aisle. "Let's get out of here," she whispered, taking his arm. The fever made her weak and she leaned on him as they walked to the front door.

A police car appeared, visible through the store's plate glass front. A male officer got out. He wasn't a Globalcop but a local police officer.

Mfumbe crouched behind a greeting-card stand, drawing Kayla down with him. The officer walked in cautiously and headed to the front of the store.

While the officer's back was turned, Kayla and Mfumbe slipped out the side door.

"There they go!" the store owner shouted.

"Come on," Mfumbe cried, grabbing her wrist and running.

"Stop!" The officer had bounded out of the store behind them. Mfumbe pushed Kayla behind him and turned to face the officer. He held his hands high.

"Run down that alley when I say 'go,'" he muttered to her. "Go!"

Kayla raced down the alley beside the store. "Stop!" the police officer shouted as she squeezed into a break in the wooden fence in the back.

Mfumbe didn't follow. She waited and still he didn't come. Heart racing, she peeked out the opening in the fence. She couldn't see Mfumbe or the officer anywhere.

LETTER TO THE EDITOR FROM NEDRA HARRIS, NATIONAL SPOKESPERSON FOR TATTOO GENERATION

Dear Editor,

Your readers may not be aware of a sad event that took place recently. Mfumbe Taylor was, until recently, a brilliant senior at Winfrey High. He was the international winner of the Virtual *Jeopardy* Tournament last year and held a full scholarship to Yale University, which he planned to attend next fall.

Mfumbe now sits in jail, accused of petty thievery. What has brought this promising young man to such a low place? Decode. Former Senator David Young's organization has helped to corrupt the minds of impressionable youth like Mfumbe, inculcating them with his paranoid belief that some sinister plot lurks behind the bar code tattoo. How ridiculous!

A further culprit in Mfumbe's downfall is a wanted criminal named Kayla Marie Reed. This young woman, also once affiliated with Decode, is wanted for the murder of her very own mother. She is also a suspect in the deaths of Mava and Toz Alan, who mysteriously crashed into a cement wall while driving Kayla to an unknown destination. How or why she caused their car to crash is still a mystery, but the young criminal remains a fugitive from justice. Mfumbe's relationship with the deeply troubled Kayla Marie Reed led him farther down the path to his current sad state.

Parents, you are the guardians of your children. Safeguard their futures. Insist that they are tattooed on their 17th birthdays. Let the example of Mfumbe Taylor demonstrate how a brilliant future can go terribly wrong without the bar code tattoo.
Sincerely,
Nedra Harris
National Spokesperson
Tattoo Generation

CHAPTER 24

Nearly delirious with fever, Kayla walked on the winding country roads for miles, heading for the town of Lake Placid, as they'd agreed. Maybe August or Allyson would show up there. But she grew so weak, she became afraid she might collapse. She feared falling right there where she might get hit, or picked up by the police, so she stepped into the woods where she followed a trail the forest service had marked with metallic-blue octagonal markers.

She pulled herself along the rocky path. Her feverish skin turned cold and clammy, and at times she felt as if it would slide off her bones. Nausea seized her, making her dizzy, and her hands trembled. She stopped to vomit, holding on to trees and rocks until nothing but liquid bile came up.

Just when she couldn't take another step, an empty lean-to appeared several yards ahead of her. She staggered to it and fell heavily inside onto its straw-covered wooden floor. Closing her eyes, she descended into a feverish sleep and lay there for two days and nights.

Wandering in restless fevered dreams, she saw

Eutonah five times. Each time, the woman had beckoned and told her to keep coming toward her. "Where are you?" Kayla heard herself say over and over. "I can't find you." Then she would open her eyes, see the pitched wooden roof of the shelter, turn, and return to her dream.

On the third day, Kayla awoke. Her mouth was parched and her head throbbed, but she was able to pull herself up to stand, then staggered out of the shelter in search of water. A pond full of jutting sticks was only yards in front of the lean-to. There was a beaver dam at the far end. The water didn't look good for drinking, but at least she could wash.

Glancing at herself in the beaver pond, she couldn't believe how she'd changed. Her hair was matted and filthy. Sharp cheekbones jutted from her thin face. Her hands had become scratched, hardened claws and her eyes were dull from sickness.

She devoured some blueberries on a nearby bush, and then reached into the pond to rinse purple juice from her stained hands. Another hand roughly gripped her wrist. Turning sharply, she looked up into piercing blue eyes of a dirty woman's face.

The woman twisted her wrist, checking for a tattoo. Seeing none, she grinned and let go. A basket of food emerged from under a flap in her torn full-length dress.

It held a hard-boiled egg, a banana, and crackers. The woman thrust the basket toward her. "Eat," she said. Kayla devoured the egg and then unpeeled the banana. Slowly, she realized that she was able to keep the food down and she no longer burned with fever.

Kayla began to cry soft tears of relief. "You came to a good place for healing," the woman said after a moment. "The earth is a constant source of energy if we use it correctly. The feeling I experience when earth energy comes to me is so joyful. These mountains, these trees — they hold a lot of really strong energy."

The only thing Kayla knew for sure was that she was well again. "Do you know where I can find a woman named Eutonah?" she asked.

The woman nodded. "I'll bring you to my group. Someone there will be able to direct you to Eutonah."

Kayla followed the woman down the trail. After several miles, the woods let out into a field. Many people sat in the tall grass, and a low murmur that reminded Kayla of buzzing bees filled the area.

"We have allies in the cosmos," the woman explained. "We are trying to channel them, to draw them into our sphere. The world needs its friends now."

A man rose from the grass and walked toward them. She knew him. "August!" she cried.

He smiled. August had also grown thinner and more muscular. When he was near enough, he clasped her hand. She noticed an ugly scar on his wrist and assumed it was where his bar code had once been. He saw her looking at it. "I made a big mistake and gave in. I see that you didn't."

"What brought you here?" she asked.

"After our last meeting, you disappeared and Mfumbe went off somewhere. Zekeal announced he was getting the tattoo. Nedra had already gotten it, and Allyson wanted her scholarship, so she got it. I couldn't see why I should hold out. I felt like everyone had deserted me. By the end of that week, I had the tattoo."

"Then what happened?" she asked.

"My parents didn't have jobs anymore, so I took one after school. It was in a biotech plant, cleaning up. One day I saw some experiments. Honestly, I had no idea what I was looking at, but the people there got super upset with me for witnessing whatever it was I saw. They told me to quit school and come live at the place as a caretaker. It was as if they wanted to own me. They said that if I didn't, they could alter my bar code so that no one else would ever want me around."

"How horrible," Kayla said, repulsed that anyone would be so cruel.

"That night I used acid to remove my code and I headed up here. I hung out around Lake Placid like we agreed, hoping you or Mfumbe would show up. But you didn't come."

"We were headed there, but we didn't make it," Kayla explained. "The police grabbed Mfumbe for shoplifting and that's the last time I saw him."

"I'll try to get to Lake Placid to see if he shows."

Kayla gripped his arm gratefully. "That would be great. I'd go to Lake Placid myself, but the Globalofficers are looking for me."

"I heard. I'm sorry about your mother."

"Thanks."

"Once I got to Lake Placid, I began to hear people talk about the different groups in the mountains. It didn't take me long to hook up with this group and I've been happy up here ever since."

"Are you trying to contact aliens?" Kayla asked skeptically.

"We're trying to attract good to help us," he answered. "We don't care where the goodness comes from. If it's aliens who respond, fine."

"She's searching for Eutonah," the woman told him.

August smiled, nodding. "Your old friend Eutonah. Do you know where she is?"

"No."

"Whiteface Mountain."

"There's such a place?" she asked.

August nodded. "It's about a day's walk from here."

It all suddenly made sense. "That's what she

meant!" Kayla realized. "Remember the white face. I didn't know it was the name of a mountain."

"Back when you mentioned it, I didn't know, either. It was once a ski resort, but there's no resort there anymore . . . just in case you were thinking of taking the chairlift up."

CHAPTER 25

It took Kayla a day to walk to the base of Whiteface Mountain. August had given her a trail map and it helped her to negotiate her way around the thick underbrush and shrubs. She had to make her way along the shore of a wide, shimmering lake before she could begin to climb.

In places the path disappeared altogether, but the map helped her estimate where she should be in relation to the lake. After a while, she veered away from the lake and came out to a meadow and a more obvious path.

Her long walk north with Mfumbe had strengthened her endurance. Her feet had grown tough and accustomed to walking. Still, she needed to stop every few miles to regain her strength. She paused and leaned against a boulder as she looked at the dirt trail ahead of her. It was surrounded on either side by tall grass dotted with flowers. The sun warmed her cheeks.

Closing her eyes, she listened to the hum of insects. She was changing, something inside was different. Having been spun out of the world she knew, she'd landed in a different world. In this world she was one living creature among many living things, not the only kind of creature in an environment of steel and glass.

Here in the woods she'd come to feel more at one with her space than she'd ever felt in her old life. There was energy in the trees, the earth, and even in the boulder she leaned on. She was aware of it these days as never before. Even when she'd lived in the cabin with Mfumbe, she hadn't been open to this feeling like she was now.

Feeling reenergized, she continued on along the narrow dirt trail through the meadow until it once again led her into the dense pine forest. The weather had grown warmer, but the coolness emanating from the thick carpet of pine needles on the forest floor still caused a chill. August had located a poncho for her and she took it from her pack and put it on.

As she hiked, she thought of Mfumbe. Was he still in jail? They couldn't keep him long just for stealing a box of Adlevenol. But had his parents come for him and taken him home? Could they force him to get tattooed?

If he was able to, she knew he'd come back and ask around for Eutonah, knowing that Kayla would also try to locate her. They'd agreed to meet in Lake Placid, but now it was too risky. Would he remember what Eutonah had said about the white face? Would August be able to find him in Lake Placid?

She had no doubt that if there was any way possible, Mfumbe would try to get to her. If he didn't, she would have to go find him. Before this, she had never known it was possible to have this kind of closeness with another person. What an unexpected gift to have received in the middle of all this misery!

August had told her that, once she started to hike the mountain, it would take only two or three hours to reach the tree line. That was where the trees grew scrubby and mostly stopped growing. From that point on, there would be only boulders to climb.

After two hours, the forest was still thick, with no sign that she would soon come above the tree line. Here and there, orange-pink light filtered through the trees, but, for the most part, the forest had become deeply shadowed.

Just ahead of her, someone moved on the trail. Her heart raced with hopeful anticipation. "Mfumbe?" she called.

He waved with a wide sweep of his arm and she ran toward him. But as she neared the figure, she skidded to a stop.

It was Zekeal, and this time he was no vision.

"Kayla!" he called, coming toward her. "I finally found you."

He was the last person she wanted to see. He'd come to bring her back to Tattoo Gen. Why else would he be here? She bolted into the woods, running as fast as she was able in the increasing darkness. He raced right behind her, closing the gap quickly. Crashing through underbrush, he leaped and caught her shoulder, pulling her to the ground with him as he fell.

Kayla kicked at him, struggling. "Get off me."

He threw himself on top of her, using his weight to pin her. "Stop! I've been looking for you ever since I arrived in Lake Placid. You never showed, so I asked around for Eutonah, figuring you'd head there. Someone finally told me. I should have known all along, the white face."

"I should never have told you that," she said.

"Listen to me. I never lied to you. I said I wasn't sure we could live without the bar code. I admitted my doubts all along."

She turned her face from him. "You were spying for Tattoo Gen all along."

"Only toward the end. I wanted to convince you all to get coded for your own sakes. You were ruining your lives."

"Why couldn't you be honest with me?"

"You were so against the bar code, so stubborn about it. I thought you'd be upset, that you'd dump me."

"I don't believe you," she jeered. "You and Nedra wanted to be big shots with Tattoo Gen — that's all there ever was to it. You tricked me and used me because you thought I was naive and would believe anything you said. Let me sit up."

"Only if you promise not to run. It's taken me too long to find you," he said, lifting himself off her.

Slowly, she sat up, eyeing him warily.

"These resistors have the wrong idea, Kayla," he said, sitting beside her. "Don't waste your time with them. They can't win."

"It's better than being a slave to Global-1," she cried heatedly.

"How is it better?" he argued. "Do you really want to be a prisoner of these mountains, unable to leave, forced to rough it in the woods? You're an artist, Kayla. What are you going to do up here in the forest for the rest of your life?"

"Live!" Kayla shouted. "Like a person, not a robot — like a *free person*."

"No, you won't," he insisted. "You'll rot up here. Come back with me. Get the tattoo. With the tattoo, you can paint and sell your work. You don't have to go to art school for that. The bar code can't take away your creativity."

He made it sound so sane, so reasonable. He stroked her hair. "Your beautiful hair. What did you do to it? It doesn't matter. Everything can be all right again, Kayla. I won't let you go this time."

Zekeal was still so handsome, so hard to resist.

But he wasn't Mfumbe. He wasn't someone who would stand up for a principle even if it wasn't in his own best interest. He wasn't Mfumbe, who would never desert her, who would do anything for her. He wasn't the person she loved from the deepest place in her heart.

"You don't believe any of what you're saying," she said. "You're not being sensible, you've just given up."

"Zekeal!" A woman hurried up the path, carrying a bright flashlight.

Kayla turned sharply toward the sound of her voice.

It was Nedra.

"You're with *her*!" Kayla whispered sharply. Everything came back to her in a cascade of bitter feeling. He'd lied to her about all of it — about Nedra, about the bar code. He'd betrayed them all, and he was doing it again. "Nothing about you has changed. You're still a liar like you always were."

"Zekeal! Where are you?" Nedra called in the dark. "I think I've found her. She left footprints."

"I don't care about her," Zekeal whispered urgently. "Now that I've found you again, I only want —"

Kayla wouldn't listen anymore. The two of them had come here to bring her back. Was there a reward for her return?

"Zekeal!" Nedra called again, louder this time. He looked toward her and Kayla shot to her feet and bolted past him, up the path.

"Kayla!" he shouted, jumping up and running after her.

She ran wildly, darting off the path. She paid no attention to direction as she scrambled over fallen trees and splashed through streams until her heart felt like it might explode. Finally, she slowed to a jog to regain her breath and slow her heart.

Several yards behind her the beam of Zekeal's flashlight careened off the trees as he searched for her in the dim light.

She stood, panting, not daring to move for fear of attracting his attention. This was a contest of wills she couldn't afford to lose. There was no way she'd let him take her back and she would never be Nedra's captive.

Several feet ahead, she heard some creature hurry away. Turning toward the sound, she saw a small cave.

She crouched low and moved stealthily to the mouth of the cave. With a quick check over her shoulder, she wriggled inside, lying flat. She knew her feet would probably have been visible in the daylight, but there was not enough room to bend her knees and pull them inside. She was grateful now for the dark — and that she had never been claustrophobic.

The cave smelled of mossy earth and the musky odor of whatever animal had inhabited it last. Dirt fell from the cave wall. She shut her eyes and spit out what fell into her mouth.

Reopening her eyes, she peered down the length of her body and out the cave opening. Zekeal moved around outside. He had stopped and, from his jerky movements, she could tell he was checking frantically for her in all directions. After about five minutes, Nedra joined him. "You let her get away," she accused him, her face demonic in the upswept light.

"No! I swear! She just disappeared."

"Keep looking. If I bring her in and get her tattooed, they'll definitely give me the council chief spot. It'll be good for you, too."

He nodded and together they hurried off into the woods, still searching. Kayla hoped that the cave was not inhabited. She didn't want to risk leaving right away, knowing Nedra and Zekeal were nearby.

She listened to the crickets chirp, along with the buzz of other insects. Lightning bugs flashed in the dark outside the cave and an owl hooted. The muscles of her calves ached and her feet throbbed. The threat of imminent danger — the adrenaline charge — was soon overcome by exhaustion and she slept.

In the middle of the night, she was abruptly awakened. She sat up, smacking her head on the upper rocks of the cave. A man's hand was wrapped around her ankle and he had begun to pull her out of the cave. "No!" she shouted, clutching at the dirt and rock at the side of the cave to no avail.

She found herself lying at the feet of a very tall man. It wasn't Zekeal or Mfumbe; she could see that much by the large shape of his silhouette. He shined a flashlight beam on her face, blinding her.

"Yes, that's her," a female voice from behind him spoke.

CHAPTER 26

Eutonah stepped into the light. She wrapped Kayla in a warm embrace. "I knew you were near. I could sense it. But when you failed to arrive, we came out to find you."

Kayla's knees buckled with relief, but she caught herself on Eutonah's arm. "We're almost at tree line," Eutonah told her. "Can you manage a short climb?"

"Yes. I think so. Is my friend Mfumbe with you?"

"Not yet, but I feel a strong energy directed toward us. Perhaps he is coming soon. Have faith. Tomorrow we will work on contacting him."

Eutonah and her group were sure-footed, even in the dark. Whenever Kayla stumbled, the large man who had pulled her from the cave steadied her with a strong hand.

They emerged from the forest to the tree line, where the plants were squat and scrubby. The moonlight made a clear path for them. A square three-story building loomed at the top of the mountain. Moonlight bounced off its many plate glass windows. "It's the old restaurant that skiers used when this was a ski resort," Eutonah told her. "It was boarded up and forgotten once they closed down the slope."

"Why did they close it?"

"It was taken over as a government headquarters and private slope for government families. Then Global-1 opened another headquarters in Hawaii and this one fell into disuse." Eutonah smiled. "Now we use it, free of charge."

Kayla followed the group through a glass door and into a vast, open space. "Our group eats together in the cafeteria, cooks in the kitchen," Eutonah explained, gesturing toward a cafeteria on her right. "We gather in the main room, and sleep in rooms we've sectioned off for ourselves. It's perfect for us."

July 21, 2025
To: (AT)cybercafe1700@globalnet.planet
From: Thefuture@globalnet.com

Amber! Are you there?

I finally have access to a computer again. I didn't even know it was here until I walked into this room just now and found it.

The last two weeks have been the most amazing of my entire life. Each day I work with our leader, Eutonah, and everyone else here on expanding our psychic abilities. We start each day with meditation in the main room. Then Eutonah assigns us to a group. She says I have a natural ability for telepathy and sensing the future, so I'm concentrating on that. I think she's right and I can't tell you how happy that makes me. Until she explained it all to me I honestly thought I was going insane. Now it explains why I was seeing Eutonah, then Zekeal. It explains why I saw a picture of Mfumbe on my sketch pad the other day.

Eutonah has been explaining such fascinating things to me. According to her and the others, Global-1 has changed the path of evolution. By cloning only the healthiest people — and making it hard for others to survive — Global-1 has stopped the course of natural human evolution.

But something unexpected has happened. People everywhere have begun developing heightened psychic ability. Many of them are here in the mountains because those are the people resisting the tattoo. Eutonah's theory is that psychic abilities are rising because people have been shut out of society as it exists.

When these people are forced out of normal ways of behaving, they find new ones. This is called adapting. Our ancient apelike ancestors adapted to a change in their physical environment. Maybe it was the Ice Age or being forced from the jungles out onto the savannas. But something made them change. They began standing on two feet to see farther and their brains grew larger because they needed to use more brainpower to survive in a harsher environment.

In the same way, we've had our social environment changed and we're adapting. Adapting in an exciting way. There's a man here who can move things with his mind. There are about fifteen women who can heal just by laying their hands on someone. This ability interests me most of all because if we are going to be shut out of medical care and killed in hospitals when we are old, then we will need healers. With people who can heal available, we won't be slaves of the insurance companies or Global-1.

After my telepathy practice today, I'll go to a class on healing with local herbs. After that, I'll learn about what plants are safe to eat around here. Eutonah says I will learn about hands-on healing when I'm ready.

In classes I'm focusing all my concentration on finding Mfumbe. I envision him at home, with his parents. I bet they came and got him out of jail and took him home with them.

I'm sure he'll try to find me. There are no phones here, so I can't call him. I could e-mail him now but I'm afraid his parents might report what they know to Global-1 or Tattoo Gen, or who knows who.

I just looked at the clock. It's time for me to go to my class right now. I hope this e-mail gets to you. I love and I miss you. I hope you're okay.

G2G,
K.

"It's all about energy," Eutonah told Kayla. They sat out by the edge of the mountain's tree line. It was the same place where Kayla had first "met" Eutonah. The woman had invited her out to talk about their work together.

"We are all part of an energy field," she said. "That's why religious figures and philosophers of all persuasions continually refer to the fact that we are all one. The whole world is one, because even the plants and animals join us on one energy continuum. Some people are more conscious of this and can control the flow of their own energy. Those people have been called holy people, swamis, medicine people, healers, saints, shamans."

"I should tell you that I've been having visions of people all converging on a walled city," Kayla said. It was hard to admit this, because she feared it revealed her emerging insanity. "There's mental illness in my family. I'm afraid this means it's starting in me."

"You're not insane," Eutonah said gently. "You are a person with strong energy flow. You're a natural conductor of energy. It's so strong in you that it can throw you forward in time and you get glimpses of the future. This extra energy flow might have driven you insane if you lived in the regular world, but you've come here, and now you're learning to harness and control your energy."

Not insane. Kayla felt as though a huge weight had been lifted from her. Not insane. "How do I learn to use my energy?" Kayla asked.

"There's a lot of work to be done," Eutonah said. "It still costs me. I feel spent afterward. This is all so new to our species, we're just starting to develop this power. You must know how to get back the energy you expend or it will drain you until there is nothing left."

"How do you get it back?"

"The earth gives it back to you. Trees do, too. Animals will share their primal energy if you are kind to them. You must stay in close contact with those things that are good and strong in your life. You must stay in touch with those people whom you love and who love you. That's what returns energy to you."

"I need to contact someone I love," Kayla said. "Mfumbe."

Eutonah gazed at Kayla, her strong, dark eyes concentrating. Then she nodded, as if she had decided something. "You begin by envisioning the person you want to contact. Focus on his image."

Kayla began to think of Mfumbe. She started with his beautiful eyes and then built his face around them. It wasn't difficult. In all the time they'd spent together, she'd memorized every plane and curve of his face until he was part of her.

The sound of footsteps broke her concentration and she saw a man hurrying down from the mountaintop. She recognized him as one of their group. He was breathless and appeared upset when he arrived. "Eutonah, I thought you should know that someone has been using the computer." The man looked at Kayla.

"Yes. It was me. I did," she admitted quickly. "I wanted to write my friend."

Eutonah and the man looked at each other.

"Did you tell your friend where you were?" Eutonah asked her.

Kayla shook her head.

"It doesn't matter," Eutonah said sadly. "They can still trace it. This location is compromised."

CHAPTER 27

Eutonah called a meeting of the entire group that evening by the large stone fireplace in the main meeting room. "Our security has been accidentally breached. It's not necessary for me to explain by whom or how. Be on alert for anything unusual. I want to use the patrol system we first set up to monitor the tree line. If anyone is coming up any face of the mountain, we want to know about it in time to either secure the building or get out."

Kayla listened, filled with guilt. Several group members turned to look at her, and Kayla was certain they knew she was to blame. She might as well confess, so she stood and spoke. "I'm so sorry."

"It's my fault. I forgot to tell you," Eutonah said. "I'm locking that room from now on. We'll keep it for emergency use only. In the meantime, let's all be extra alert and get the patrols up and running."

For the next five days, all lessons were suspended, since no one seemed able to concentrate. Kayla sat alone on her sleeping bag working on sewing together a jacket of animal pelts left over from when the group hunted its meals.

The group often argued over whether they should eat meat or not. Kayla didn't eat meat anymore, suddenly finding she preferred nuts, berries, greens, and eggs. But she was glad some of them did eat meat and knew how to prepare the skins. She'd been told that the winter would be bitterly cold, and she didn't want to be caught without a coat or jacket.

By August the patrol was dropped. The group felt that Kayla's e-mail hadn't put them in danger after all and was once again fully concentrated on perfecting their telepathic skills. Kayla kept her mind focused on Mfumbe, and each day her ability to "see" him increased.

When she closed her eyes and concentrated on an image of his face now, it soon gave way to a picture of him that she suspected showed her what he was doing. Sometimes she saw him in a car, sometimes on the side of a road. *Come to me*, she said in her mind. *I'm waiting for you. Keep coming toward me.*

It took all her strength to contact him. Each time she'd sleep for nearly twelve hours afterward. She was overjoyed each time she felt the deep exhaustion because it proved to her that she'd really made contact. Eutonah encouraged her to sleep outside, "where you can be replenished by earth energy."

Kayla was napping outside on the ground one August afternoon. She was right near the end of the forest just below the tree line, where large pines gave way to small ones. A branch snapped.

Still caught in sleep, she turned groggily toward the sound. The sun shone in her eyes. Black silhouettes moved toward her.

She came more fully awake and squinted into the sun. There were about six figures approaching and they were all dressed in the same style of jumpsuit.

Maybe they're from another resistance group, she thought, pulling forward to sitting. She repositioned herself out of the sun's glare where she could see better. Her heart raced and she was suddenly energized by fear. The woman approaching her was Nedra Harris. She sprang to her feet and began to run, legs pumping hard.

A loud cracking sound exploded in her ear seconds before searing pain exploded her shoulder and shot through her entire body, throwing her to the ground.

Her shoulder!

She'd been shot in her shoulder.

Pressing her forehead to the ground, she waited for a second shot to finish her. But the group raced past, their footsteps pounding in her ears. They were running up toward the building on top of the mountain.

Then she heard another man approaching from behind. The pain coursing through her body made it impossible to turn. Her entire body tensed as she waited for a final bullet. She pressed her cheek to the cool dirt, shut her eyes, and waited.

The man put his hand on her waist, but with surprising gentleness. "Oh, my God," he murmured.

Opening her eyes, she faced Mfumbe.

Her mouth opened with words of love and joy at seeing him. All that came out was a rush of air.

"It's okay. It's okay," he whispered, looking for a way to lift her.

Shots rang out from the building above them; screams and shouting and more shots. Mfumbe slid his arms under her body and lifted. "Okay?" he asked.

She nodded, grinding her teeth against the crushing pain.

Someone in a jumpsuit scrambled down the mountaintop toward them. He held a rifle high. "Stop!" he ordered them.

"It's Zekeal," Mfumbe told her in an undertone as he kept moving slowly backward toward the trees. Kayla guessed he was hoping to disappear into the forest behind them.

Zekeal called to a suited figure up by the building. "I have them." He turned back and aimed his gun at them. "Put her down, Mfumbe."

"She's badly hurt," Mfumbe told him.

"Put her down and come with me. I'll send some people down to get her."

Kayla tried to object, but her voice was too dry and low for them to hear. She dug her fingers into Mfumbe's arm and shook her head.

Mfumbe's eyes darted between Kayla and

Zekeal as he lowered her carefully to the ground. "What happened to you?" he asked Zekeal. "I thought Dave Young was your guy. I thought you were going to stand strong against this."

What was Mfumbe doing? Was he really letting Zekeal bring them in? He must think she was so injured it was his only choice. And he was probably right. What else could they do? But it seemed unreal that they had come this far only to be brought in by Tattoo Gen.

Zekeal kept his rifle trained on Mfumbe. "Shut up," he replied. "Dave Young is on his way down, just like the rest of you. I tried to help you both, but it's too late for that now."

Up at the building, another gunshot fired. Someone screamed.

Zekeal glanced up, distracted by the sounds. In that moment, Mfumbe leaped at him, knocking Zekeal backward. His gun fell, bouncing once and discharging a shot as it hit the ground.

Kayla recoiled at the sound. This was her chance to escape, but pain had made her helpless, too weak to get up and run.

The rifle slid toward Kayla, stopping just out of her reach. She stretched toward it and the effort sent searing knifelike pain up her injured arm.

Zekeal and Mfumbe were locked in their fight, both tumbling over and over toward trees at the edge of the forest. Zekeal landed on top and began to punch Mfumbe, smashing him hard in the face.

Over them, a half-dead pine creaked in the breeze. A thick pine branch dropped brown needles on the fight below it. Kayla watched the branch dangle dangerously above the two of them.

She shut her eyes and envisioned the tree branch. With every bit of her remaining strength she saw the branch in all its detail.

She felt where it was weak, on the verge of splitting. She absorbed that image of weakness, made it a part of her.

That's where she focused her own energy.

Her total energized being aimed itself at that weak spot in the branch — aimed at cracking it. Kayla tossed her head back with the effort of total focus. Her own power coursed through her as she concentrated the entire strength of her being on energy release.

With her head thrown back, she didn't see the branch sail through the air, tumbling down through the levels of branches, end over end. But she heard the sickening crunch of bones breaking as it landed.

CHAPTER 28

Fall came early to the Adirondacks. By the end of September, orange and yellow dotted the mountains and a chill swept through the pines, heightening their smell and making them sway majestically. Kayla was aware of the change as she made her way down the mountainside, holding a letter she hoped would reach Amber.

She was running slightly behind schedule and quickened her pace. At the bottom of the mountain she still had to make her way along the narrow dirt path that led to the dock on the lake. There, a man in a speedboat would wait to take her letter and the twenty other letters she'd received from resisters in the mountains to their intended destinations.

He was part of a secret organization called "the postmen" who collected mail and delivered it to other "postmen." The mail was secretly passed until it reached the person it was intended for. It was a way of avoiding e-mail, which could be so easily tracked by Global-1. They came to the dock once a week, but always at different times. Kayla was the one designated to meet the postman this week and she didn't want to miss him.

She thought of Amber, isolated out west, with only her strung-out family and crazy cousin. In the weeks since she and Mfumbe had escaped the Tattoo Gen raid, the resistance groups had scattered, then slowly re-formed and made contact with one another. These days Mfumbe and Kayla lived in an abandoned hunting cabin. Her wound was slowly healing since a doctor from August's group had removed the bullet, though her shoulder now ached horribly before every rainfall.

Although they were on their own, Kayla felt part of a caring community in a way she had never experienced in her old neighborhood. People left messages under rocks and communicated in coded imitations of animal calls. Mostly, though, they contacted one another with their minds. Telepathy had become commonplace here in the mountains. There was no need to travel when a face could be mentally conjured and a message received.

As she hiked, she felt a familiar surge of energy in her mind. Experience had taught her to stop and slow her breathing.

Eutonah stepped out from behind a thick pine ahead of her. "Hello, my dear friend," she greeted her.

"You're alive," Kayla said in a voice thick with relief. She hadn't known what had become of Eutonah after the raid.

"I'm in a prison that Global-1 operates, but I'm

also with you," Eutonah told her. "My spirit can't be imprisoned, so I go where I choose."

"We have to free you," Kayla said.

"David Young is organizing in Washington. We have to support him. It's time to stop hiding up here in the mountains. He needs our help."

Kayla cringed when she heard Eutonah's words. The idea of returning to the "civilized" world filled her with dread. Back there she'd known death, loneliness, lies, and betrayal. She was happier here than she'd ever been in her entire life. She looked away from Eutonah, trying to get hold of her emotions. She looked back in time to see the woman's image fade.

Kayla sat on the rickety narrow dock on a secluded inlet of the lake. She placed a rock on top of her letters to keep them from blowing away and waited for the postman. Sun bounced off the water, shimmering, throwing off glimmering light. She stared into it and the lights dazzled and danced before her eyes . . .

*   *   *

They are inside the white city now. A man stands at a podium. She remembers his face from pictures. David Young speaks to the crowd. Thousands of people stand around a long, low pool and listen. She is with Mfumbe. David Young tells the crowd to focus on a world where people move freely. Unafraid. He tells them to envision a world of equality and justice where all are valued, regardless of their genetic code. "We will not use violence to achieve our ends," he says. "But we can use the strength and energy of our minds to change our world."

She and Mfumbe join the crowd to envision this new world. The deeper they go, the tighter she and Mfumbe hold hands, determined to make their vision a reality.

*   *   *

The sound of the boat's engine woke her from her vision. She blinked hard to come fully back, then waved to the postman as he cut the engine and let the boat drift up to the dock. "Great day, isn't it?" he said as she handed him the bundle of letters. He glanced at the letter to Amber right on top. "This one has a long journey ahead of it," he commented.

"Amber Thorn is my best friend. All I know is that she's in Nevada, somewhere outside of Carson City."

"I bet this gets to her," he said. "More than ever before, people are helping us. It'll keep getting passed along until it reaches someone who knows her. All across the country, people are getting fed up with Global-1 and Loudon Waters."

"That's encouraging," she said.

He smiled at her. "Yeah, it is."

He started his engine and waved as he headed back across the lake. She returned his wave, then began her hike home to the cabin.

How could she go back to the regular world? Here in the mountains she'd been able to start sketching again, using burned wood from their fires. She was doing drawings of the wildlife all around and her work was the best she'd ever done. *I've become myself here*, she realized. If she went back, would she be able to hold on to that true self?

When she returned home two hours later, Mfumbe and August sat outside the cabin, cross-legged, talking. Mfumbe held an open paper on his lap. From the way they kept glancing at it, she assumed they were talking about something written on it. "What's that?" she asked.

"Young is calling for a major rally," August replied. "He wants everyone in the country opposed to the bar code to attend. I don't see what he's going to accomplish."

"People all over the country are changing," Mfumbe argued. "Kayla and I barely speak out loud to each other anymore. We use our minds to communicate. I think it's an evolutionary change that's happened quickly because the bar code has changed our environment so dramatically that we've had to adapt."

"I see what you mean. Our group is the same," August conceded. "We barely speak."

"Don't you see, then?" Mfumbe insisted. "This — what we're living here — this is the new world, not the Global-1 world. Young has a coalition of senators and other leaders behind him. They've laid out a whole package of new laws that would give back all sorts of rights and freedoms, including the freedom to live without the bar code tattooed on your wrist."

Kayla listened, thinking — remembering what Eutonah had said about going back, remembering her vision. "Global-1 is going to fight back with all it's got," she commented. She thought of the aerial bombing she'd seen in her vision.

Did they really have to go back to all that misery? She remembered the raid by Tattoo Gen. Global-1 and Tattoo Gen were powerful and ruthless.

"We call ourselves the resisters," Mfumbe continued. "But we should really call ourselves the hiders. That's all we're doing up here, hiding."

August got to his feet. "I disagree with you there," he said. "We've grown strong up here. We know who we are now. Think about what we were, five people in a warehouse, and two of them were spies. Now we're strong and united."

"But we're *hiding*," Mfumbe insisted. "And besides, there are bound to be more raids. We can't just sit here and wait for them to come for us."

"We could go to Canada," August suggested.

"We could," Kayla agreed. But more than anything, she wanted to stay here.

"I have to go back for supper," August said. "See you both."

When August disappeared into the trees, Mfumbe turned to Kayla. He switched into their wordless telepathic way of communicating mind-to-mind. *It happened. I had a vision like the visions you have*, Mfumbe told her with his mind. *You and I were with lots of people from the mountains and other places. We were heading toward the capital to confront Loudon Waters and Global-1. They attacked us, even fired on us, but we kept going. We were all communicating with our minds and we were unstoppable. Dave Young was holding elections for freely elected people who weren't controlled by Global-1.*

Kayla grabbed his arm. She was too unnerved by the thought of going back to speak with her mind. "I can't do it," she said desperately. "I've been so happy here. I was so miserable there."

He drew her to him and held her tenderly. "We'll be together, always together. Now that our minds can touch, nothing can part us."

Being parted from him again was one of her fears. Was it true that they could always find each other now? Eutonah had found her. Maybe it *was* true.

Lee, the gray cat they'd found in the forest, raced out of the trees. He had something in his mouth and was heading for her. "Oh, no!" she gasped. He had a small black-and-white bird, a chickadee.

He laid it at her feet, nearly dead. One of its wings hung limply, unhinged, and it shivered.

"Oh, God. Poor bird," Mfumbe sympathized, standing beside her. The bird stopped shivering and lay there, still.

Kayla picked up the small creature and covered it in her hands. Walking away from Mfumbe, she imagined her hands becoming warm with her own life energy. She shut her eyes and imagined the energy as being blue, then she directed the stream of blue into the bird. She did this until her knees began to quiver. Still, she kept directing the energy. Streaks of various colors shot like fireworks in the darkness behind her eyelids. Her entire body trembled.

And in her hands something stirred. The smallest fluttering of a wing.

Uncupping her hands, she saw the bird's chest gently rising and falling.

It looked at her, then righted itself and flew to the nearest branch. After resting there a moment, it rose up and soared through the blue Adirondack sky.

Mfumbe wrapped his arms around her. Completely spent of energy, she slumped against him. "Amazing," he said softly.

Tears of exhaustion and joy welled in her eyes. Despite her fatigue, she had never felt so strong.

"Where do you suppose he's going?" Mfumbe said.

"Home," she replied, somehow certain. "Going home." The word *home* resonated inside her and she thought of the song her mother used to sing.

I'm like a bird, I only fly away. . . .

Those words weren't true for her anymore. She'd found her power and her soul. And her home was inside her. There was no bar code on her wrist, and she felt proud of that. She hadn't given herself over to anything that would control or diminish her — not to Zekeal, not to Global-1. She'd protected herself and Mfumbe by breaking a branch with her mind, and she would use the power of her mind again.

She looked up at Mfumbe. "All right. I think we can do this," she said. "I'll go back. I've seen a vision and I see us winning. It's worth risking everything."

AUTHOR'S NOTE

How I Came to Write *The Bar Code Tattoo*

THE END IS NEAR! That's what the flyer in my hands said. In fact, it gave the exact date and time. My friend Mary had just flown in from Texas that day and someone had handed the paper to her in the airport. Now she handed it to me as a joke. "Very funny," I said.

Later, though, I read it more carefully. The reason for this coming cataclysm, it went on to say, was that the prophecies as laid out in the biblical book of Revelations were about to be fulfilled. The last fulfillment was that Europe was about to be united and everyone would be branded with a bar code. The guideposts of the bar code were equivalent to the mark of the devil. Without the "mark of the devil" no one would be able to buy or sell. That's what got me thinking. If you couldn't buy or sell, you'd really be in big trouble.

The date for "the end" came and went. But I was still thinking about buying and selling. The implications led me to write a piece of short fiction that was essentially the story of the Thorn family. But that story made me wonder what kind of info would be contained in the bar code. While I was pondering this, the Human Genome project was going on and — while I was thinking about *that* — Nelly Furtado was singing her plaintive song on the radio. Suddenly, everything everywhere seemed relevant to the story developing inside me. It all poured itself into Kayla's journey — and I guess that's a pretty fair description of the creative process. At any rate, it's the story of how I came to write *The Bar Code Tattoo*.

—Suzanne Weyn